The King of Desolation

Book One of The Ballad of Gods and Men

Mayson Kukwa

This One's For You, Papaw Kook. You will forever be in my thoughts.

Prologue

"We should get back," Lady Vigdis urged them as an army marched in from their right. "The Harayuma bloodline is dead."

"Yes, that might be true, but their army still outranks ours, M'lady," Randel said right before he started to bite his nails.

"Does the fact that we killed an entire bloodline frighten you?" said Lord Torlief with a hint of a smile on his face.

Randel did not take the bait; he was a young boy in his twenties, but he knew better than to take Lord Torlief's bait. "The dead are dead, my Lord; we have no reason to fear the dead."

Lady Vigdis got on her horse. "We ride north, back to the northern point of Eldandoor," said Lady Vigdis as she jumped on her horse.

"Have you gone mad, M'lady? We'll never reach Eldandoor before the Harayuma army flanks us," Randel said, not meaning to question her authority but out of genuine fear for his life.

Lady Vigdis fought alongside Lord Viper, the king of Eldandoor. She was almost positive that if she and her party made it into the walls of Eldandoor before the Harayuma army caught them, they would be safe; they might even have a chance to fight back and eradicate the Harayuma army.

"The Harayuma army lacks two vital things: the first being allies. Nobody in the Realm of Nastomar wants to be allied with not only a small empire but one that has already been burned to the ground. The second is a commander, and we killed every single war commander and strong fighter in Ember Fall. The Harayuma army is just a bunch of weak followers of a dead bloodline. If we ride to Eldandoor, we can get the resources to fight back. Now get on your horse or die like a coward," said Lady Vigdis with a smidge of anger in her eyes.

The two other members of Lady Vigdis's party got on their horses and rode about sixteen miles north, making it to the outer walls of Eldandoor. It was an area filled with hill-like land and places to hide, but the kingdom itself was built on a plain. Just as the sun began to set, the rest of the Harayuma army rode close behind. The drawbridge rose as they reached the wall, and the gates closed.

"Eldandoor seeks no refugees," an older man with a crossbow said from on top of the wall. He had a long, scraggly beard and a large scar across his face.

"We are the farthest thing from refugees. I am Lady Vigdis, and I demand that you open the gate; I must have a word with Lord Viper."

Lord Viper walked out of the front gate with a torch in his hand. "Lady Vigdis, you may not enter. We may have supported you in your last battle against Mystria, but you are nothing but a whore wearing shiny armor." Lord Viper had gone mad with the power of the largest army in the four kingdoms in the south.

As the gate closed for the second time, the Harayuma army closed in on the party. "Please, we beg you to let us in! We will die without your support," said Randel as he drew his sword.

"Put your sword down, boy!" said Lord Torleif. The Harayuma was right behind them. There was nothing Lady Vigdis could do—neither Lord Torleif nor the poor Randel.

"We yield. Do not take our lives. We will do anything," said Lady Vigdis.

"I see you attempted to destroy not only my home but my family as well, Lady Vigdis, although it seems as if you missed one." Kaito Harayuma jumped off his horse and walked towards the party. "I seek no harm, not yet, at least. I am angered by the fact you thought you could get away with destroying Ember Fall. I will kill every single one of you, but that's not what I am seeking at the moment. What I do seek is the princess of Eldandoor, yes, the same one Lord Viper has locked in the crypt. Now you can either fight alongside me or be another life I take on the journey for immortality."

As he said that, four of Kaito's men put Lady Vigdis, Randel, and Lord Torlief in rope cuffs and put them in the back of Kaito's army. "Now, Lord Viper, give me the princess or die," said Kaito.

"Men, grab the Lady from the keep. It's not worth the fight," said Lord Viper.

Lady Liv, a tall blonde-haired lady, walked out of the gates alongside her father. Once Liv was safe in the army beside Kaito, Kaito pulled out a crossbow and shot Lord Viper directly in the heart. "That one is for treating my men like trash," he said as he shot Viper. He shot two more shots. "And those two are for enslaving my people and betraying our trust."

"Are you alright, M'lady?"

"Yes, m'Lord, thank you for the rescue," said Lady Liv.

It was almost like Kaito was a hero, saving Lady Liv from a soon-to-be mad king, but it was nothing more than a plot of power for Kaito Harayuma.

The Duality of Man

Man is built from two essential parts: love and power. Both become a powerful whirlwind inside the body of man.

Men like Lord Viper seek out power and violence, while men like Kaito Harayama seek out power and love. Kaito Harayuma's army was far from the greatest army. The whole Harayuma bloodline was constructed of noble blacksmiths and cooks.

"It's no longer safe in Eldandoor or Frost Fall, nor is it safe in Ember Fall. M'lady, we have one choice. We must set up camp a few miles away from shore, and we shall build our kingdom. What do you say to this?" asked Kaito.

"I say it's not a very bright idea, but we must do it," said Lady Liv, the last of her bloodline. "You heard her, men, start setting up camp tonight; we shall move towards the shore in the west at dawn."

Over the next three hours, the night began to settle, and a camp had formed. Kaito had gone towards the imprisonment tent in which the three prisoners sat.

"Lady Vigdis, I would like a word with you." Kaito unchained her and brought her outside for a walk by lantern light. "This is a new opportunity for you. You were a knight for Ember Fall, yet you betrayed my people's trust. This is the opportunity to pledge yourself back to the Harayuma bloodline yet again and serve as my knight, my war commander. I know you have battle experience. After all, you wouldn't have been able to kill all of Ember Fall without a strategic plan. So what do you say? Pledge your allegiance to the Harayuma bloodline once more."

"I shall do this under one condition: you allow Lord Torlief to be your advisor and Rendal to live within this new kingdom you are building," said Lady Vigdis with sincerity in her eyes.

"I shall do it, but there is something you must know: an elder of Ember Fall has promised me immortality if I wed and have a child with Lady Liv. She is truly a gorgeous woman, but I must convince her to wed me and become my queen," said Kaito with determination in his eyes.

Lady Vigdis and Kaito went their separate ways. Before Kaito returned to his tent, Lady Liv walked up to him.

"How about a walk before bed?" said Lady Liv.

"Why, that sounds lovely, Liv," Kaito said, feeling the nerves from speaking to such a lovely woman.

"So Kaito, why did you decide to save me?" Lady Liv asked with a happy and excited demeanor.

"Well, my Lady, if I'm being utterly honest, you are gorgeous. Do you remember the ball when we were just children? My parents fought hard to gain access to that ball, and even then, I recognized your beauty from across the room. Also, an elder from Ember Fall said if I truly fell in love with you, my family line would be granted immortality."

"Yes, I do remember the ball. I always thought you were handsome for such a noble bloodline. It is a shame what Lady Vigdis did to your people," said Lady Liv, clinging to

Kaito's arm. "You know, we are now both at the end of our bloodlines. Nobody else can carry our names." Lady Liv said with the love in her eyes.

"That is true, Liv, but you must know, we carry a burden now to save our bloodlines from certain death, m'lady. Do you know how to fight?" asked Kaito with a sudden change from determination to excitement.

"Why no, I do not. But I truly would love to learn. Will you teach me?" asked Liv with a sudden burst of joy.
"I would love to teach you, but first, we must get some rest before our journey west at dawn. I have a tent for you near my new knight, Lady Vigdis. You may sleep there for the night," said Kaito with a tad bit of tiredness in his heart.

"Kaito, I want to sleep in your tent. I would feel safer that way," said Lady Liv.

Kaito nodded in agreement, and they slept in the same bed for the first time together.

A New Start

Lady Liv had awoken before Kaito, but she knew how important riding west was to their survival, so she woke him up.

"Hey, sleepyhead, it's time to get up. We must ride west, remember?" she said, smiling from ear to ear. She thought to herself, "This could be the one."

As Kaito walked out of the tent, he grabbed his sword. He nicknamed it Shadowblade, as it was made of dark steel, making the sword black, more black than obsidian. Kaito and his three hundred men rode west until noon, when they found a forest near the shore.

"This is where we shall build our kingdom. You all know what to do!" said Kaito.

Lord Torlief walked up to Kaito. "You know this makes you a king. Look, I'm sorry for what happened in Ember Fall."

"A great war is upon us, Torleif. If we do not build our armies soon, the Harayuma and the Viper bloodlines will die." Kaito said this with the utmost fear in his eyes. He knew if he survived, he would have to build fast. He stood no chance with only three hundred men to his name; he had to ally with someone, somehow.

"Bring me Lady Liv and Lady Vigdis. Tell them to meet me in the command tent."

"Yes, my Lord."

Five minutes passed, and Lady Liv, Lord Kaito, and Lady Vigdis sat around a table of the four kingdoms.

"We must go to Mystria. If we seek out an alliance with their people, we might just have a chance at this, and Queen Saga might have what we need to survive the upcoming winter. Lady Vigdis, you must watch over our new kingdom as I and Lady Liv leave for Mystria." Kaito said, gripping the arm of his chair in determination.

"Why must I go, Kaito?" asked Lady Liv very curiously.

"You are now the queen of a new kingdom, and you must follow your king wherever he goes," Lady Vigdis said with a bolt of excitement.

"We leave in a week. That gives us time to practice our fighting skills. You do want to learn, Liv, don't you?"

"Yes, my king, when can we start?"

"Meet me at our tent at nightfall. We shall start then," said Kaito with excitement. Dusk hit the kingdom, and the bell rang. Everyone went to their tents for the night except for Lady Liv and Kaito.

"Alright, plant your feet about six inches apart," says Kaito. "Alright, now raise your sword. And swing."

For her first lesson, she was able to knock Kaito down, but she didn't have enough training to hurt him badly. After their training, they went to bed and lay in the same bed for a second time. When they awoke in the morning, they knew what journey lay ahead. Kaito grabbed his sword beside his tent and began walking to their horses with Lady Liv.

"Do I get my horse?" asked Lady Liv in excitement. "I have barely ridden a horse, my king."

"You could always ride on the back of mine, and it is a straight shot to Mystria. I am sure we will have no trouble, a three-day venture there and back." Kaito grinned. Seeing Liv so excited made him feel like his duty as a king was fulfilled. Liv had decided to ride her own horse; after all, she loved the animal and wanted to learn more to help her king.

The first three hours were calm, and nothing had happened until they began to ride through what was known as the dead city. Walking through the dead city was the quickest way to Mystria. However, if caught, they would be hung and burned from the trees surrounding them by the Knights of the Red Death. The guards who protected the dead city, inside the dead city, were an army of the dead that killed anyone and everyone inside. The knights didn't stick around the dead city often, only patrolling once or twice a year, though. Kaito did not think anything of it, completely forgetting the horror stories of the city from his childhood.

The air grew thick around them suddenly, and in the blink of an eye, they were surrounded by 100 men, half of whom were archers and the other half being fully armored knights. Kaito knew what choices lay before him: try and make peace with the devilish knights or fight for the lives of his people.

"Stay behind me, Liv. This might get nasty."

Kaito and Liv stood back-to-back in combat for the first time. Kaito had his dark steel sword in hand, Liv with her shortsword. The knights began marching, circling Kaito and Liv, preparing for a bloody fight. The first man rushed towards Kaito, and with sheer speed, Kaito blocked the knight's attack with the blade of his sword. The knight was stunned, but Kaito saw this as the perfect strike opportunity. He threw his sword forward with the force of a giant, and it went straight through the armor and out the back of the knight's body.

The knights did not back off. Instead, a knight rushed towards Liv, and without even thinking, Liv threw her sword forward, piercing through the knight's skull.
"Nice one, Liv, but don't let it get to your head. There is plenty more blood to be spilled."

Three more knights ran forward toward Kaito, but he stood no chance. Two of the men struck simultaneously, while the other arm of Kaito blocked the third swing. Kaito's dark steel sword went flying in the air. The fight had been lost, or so they had thought. From the distance, Kaito heard the sound of horses galloping through. Screaming erupted over the battlefield as five men, all wearing the sigil of Eldandoor Kingdom, distracted the knights. Within seconds, the tide of battle had switched. Kaito grabbed his sword and Lady Liv, putting her on his horse.

"We must leave at once," Kaito said with grace in his eyes. "The gods have saved us this time, but I am sure we won't be as lucky next time."

Kaito and Liv continued their journey through the night, making it to a small town known as Rivers Keep. They had made it about halfway to Mystria.

Frost Fall

Word of the extermination of the Harayuma bloodline had spread across The Sea of The Dragon all the way to Frost Fall. But so did the word of King Viper's assassination. Aislinn was a firm believer in anarchy and justice. Not for a single day did she follow the rules of any god or kingdom. She was intrigued by Kaito Harayuma. Not only by the fact that he survived the destruction of his family but by the fact that he rose against his oppressors, killing the soon-to-be mad king and taking his enemies captive. Her family were low-class farmers, but Aislinn had secretly been practicing the way of underhanded combat. At nightfall, Aislinn snuck out of the farmer's hut in her village, which just so happened to be near the Frost Fall docks. As she snuck away, she went to a nearby grave and dug up a silk pouch of coin. She opened the silk pouch and swiftly counted them to make sure she had enough coins. As she neared the docks, she was met by an old wise man.

"I have the money. We leave for the north immediately," she said with a thrill in her voice. The older man took and counted the money before boarding a small fishing ship. The trip would not be long, only a day or two, depending on the weather. Before Aislinn knew it, the boat began to cut through the dark waters of The Sea of The Dragon, leaving the bright lights of Frost Fall behind. Aislinn stood at the edge of the deck, feeling the cool sea breeze. Driven by her rebellious spirits and the allure of the unknown, the wise older man, a weathered figure with piercing eyes and a long gray beard, navigated the vessel with a steady hand.

As the boat sailed further into the night, Aislinn couldn't help but feel a mix of excitement and trepidation. The moonlight cast a reflection off of the gentle waves, casting an ethereal glow upon the sea. During the first day of the journey, Aislinn spent most of her time observing the crew as they shared tales of their past adventures on the waters. One of the men had lost his eye fighting his nephew, and another crew member had lost his finger in a blacksmithing accident. Their stories lit Aislinn up with excitement. Aislinn listened intently, absorbing the lore of the distant lands and the man-beasts they called humans. The wise older man saw her curiosity, sat down beside her, and began sharing his own stories, weaving the tales of an ancient prophecy and the lost civilization.

The second day brought many challenges as the weather started to become more unpredictable. Massive dark clouds loomed overhead, and the sea grew restless. Aislinn, determined to prove herself a capable member of the crew, helped the wise old man and the rest of the crew with many tasks, learning to tie several different types of knots; they even jokingly taught her how to tie a noose. She learned how to secure the sails. The ship began to rock back and forth with the rhythm of the waves, testing the mettle of not only the ship but its passengers as well. As the ship sailed through rough waters, the wise old man approached Aislinn, his eyes filled with a mixture of wisdom and concern. He gave invaluable advice on weathering storms and navigating the turbulent seas, emphasizing the critical components of resilience and adaptability.

By the end of the second day, the boat had reached its destination, a secluded northern port where whispers of rebellion and resistance echoed in the air. Aislinn disembarked, her heart pounding with anticipation for the many challenges that lay ahead of her. The wise old man bid her farewell.

A Very Warm Welcome

Kaito and Liv leave RiverFall at dawn, making it to the outer civilization of Mystria by mid-day. When they had gotten to the walls, a tall, fat man walked out of the walls.

"Ah yes, you must be the new king of Ember Fall." He seemed nervous to be in the grace of such a mighty king.

"Ember Fall has fallen, nothing left but dust and stone," Kaito says with a disappointed look on his face.

"I am Sir Gordan Maccances, and I am here to lead you to Queen Saga. She has been waiting for your arrival for quite some time." Sir Gordon bowed to Queen Liv and King Kaito.

Sir Gordon led the party through Mystria, a beautiful place this time of year. The trees are orange and beginning to lose their leaves, the climate is nice and warm, and the air smells like freshly baked pies. Liv taps Kaito on the shoulder and looks up, and so does Kaito. In front of them is the largest castle in all the kingdoms. Mystria was once the most prominent kingdom before King Niall was killed in battle against his people. Since then, most people have either sought a home elsewhere or continued to agree that the Lords and Ladies of Mystria were otherworldly, magical beings.

"Well, here it is, the throne room. I wish you two the utmost luck." Sir Gordon smiled and walked off.

"Lord Kaito, I see you brought a visitor with you," says Queen Saga, her legs crossed in her chair. Lady Saga was a Lady in her mid-thirties with long red hair. Around her chair lay the heads of three wolves.

"Yes, Your Grace, this is Lady Liv of Eldandoor." Liv bowed and said, "Your Grace, I have heard much about you. It is truly an honor."

"Yes, well, now is not the time for small talk, Kaito. What is it you seek in Mystria?"

"Your Grace, we seek help through the winter. My home in Ember Fall has been burnt to the ground. My men and I are living in a remote woodland off the shore in the west. I did pledge my allegiance to Ember Fall, but seeing as it is now a rotten pit in the ground, that doesn't matter. Kaito, you are the last of your bloodline, and for that, I respect you. We shall send food, money, and resources to your new home in the woods." Lady Saga said, welcoming Kaito into her kingdom.

"I do ask one favor of you: continue your bloodline, rebuild your kingdom, and when you do. I expect you to be a mighty king, and you, Lady Liv, I expect you to be a just and loving queen, not only for your people but for your king who stands beside you."

"Yes, Your Grace," both Kaito and Liv said as they bowed.

Kaito and Liv were very tired from their long journey to Mystria. So they were given a room in the inn for the night, and they were set to leave with a dozen new citizens to their town and a bunch of resources as well. In the room was a bed, a couch, and a table. Lady Liv had gone out to get some food to eat before they went to bed. And when she arrived back, they dug into an excellent Mystria cherry pie.

A Grand Discovery.

Aislinn had just gotten off the ship, stepping onto new land for the first time. She was met by a young man sitting at the docks.

"Do you know where I can find Kaito Harayuma?" asked Aislinn.

"I believe I do, and to you, that would be King Kaito. He rode to Mystria not so long ago, but he will be back by tomorrow. I could show you the way to the new empire if you'd like," said the young man. He couldn't be any more than sixteen, around the same age as Aislinn.

"Thank you, kind sir, it would be an honor to come with you." They both hopped on horses and rode towards the unnamed empire. When they got there, walls had already begun to be built. The resources Queen Saga gave them boosted their building tenfold.

"By all that is holy, this has become quite a town," said Aislinn. She had a sense of excitement and was extremely excited.

"What can I say? The king has a gifted talent." Aislinn had begun to walk amongst the town folk. It wasn't a small town, but it wasn't big yet, either. The air tasted of pine and sweet potatoes. Towards the end of town was Rendal, working as a blacksmith to show his gratitude towards Lady Vigdis and Kaito.

Aislinn walked up to Rendal, "I'm Aislinn. It's very nice to meet you."

"The name's Rendal, it's an honor to meet such a beauty like you." Rendal had joy in his voice. He may have betrayed the Harayuma bloodline, but he was joyful to have a brand new start in his life, away from the wrongdoings he had done in the past.

"Say, Rendal, do you have any spare iron or steel?" asked Aislinn, looking to get a pair of daggers made for herself. She had spent three years practicing and now believes she can put her skills to use, hunting, farming, and, best of all, killing under the Harayuma reign.

"Why yes, I have enough iron to last a fortnight. I will make you something once you get yourself some gold," Rendal says with a grin on his face. He knew he could have easily made the pretty girl something without her paying, but he wanted to become a richer and more powerful person. Lady Vigdis and Lord Torlief had noticed the young Lady Aislinn. They took the opportunity to introduce themselves and find out what she had come for. After all, the status between Eldandoor and the Kaito Harayuma Empire was not in good grace.

"Hello, young Lady, I am Lady Vigdis. I am the king's knight and war commander; the man beside me is Lord Torlief, King Kaito's most trusted advisor."

"I am Aislinn Willdarde and I come from Frost Fall to meet your king."

"Know what a noble Lady like you wants with the king, and why come so far to meet such a new king?" asked Lord Torlief, confused at why a young Lady would come so far to meet a king that hasn't even been king for more than a week.

"Your Lord, if I may say, I have heard many tales of Kaito Harayuma. I have been told he is the king slayer, the last surviving son of his family, and not only that, I have been told he is a god amongst men. Now I believe in no such thing as a god, but if all the tales are true, I would love to fight alongside such a man," Aislinn said this in such a truthful way that Lady Vigdis and Lord Torlief left her be.

Aislinn grabbed a bow and some arrows from the archery range and left for the woods to hunt, not only to help the town but to make some gold for herself. When she got deep enough into the woods, she saw a piece of ore, an ore that was rumored to have been destroyed thousands of years ago. Only six or seven weapons were made with this one. She shoved the ore into her pocket and continued moving. She heard the sounds of crunching leaves in the distance. She stood still, loading her bow and aiming in the direction of the noise, and out walked a huge elk, one of the biggest she had ever seen. She aimed her bow and shot it straight through the heart, leaving it no time to move out of the way. She grabbed the legs of the elk and dragged it through the woods all the way back to the butcher.

"By all the gods, this could feed our whole army!" shouted the butcher excitedly. "I assume you want to be paid. Here is a hundred gold; don't go spend it all in one place," the butcher said as he put the gold coins into Aislinn's hands.

Her next stop was Rendal's stall. When she got there, she told Rendal, "I have found emberite, Rendal!"

"There's no chance in hell you found emberite. There's no such thing," Rendal said before Aislinn pulled the ore out of her pocket.

"Here it is. I'll give you a hundred gold if you keep this between us and make me a pair of daggers out of it," Aislinn said, trying to keep her voice down.
"Consider it done, M'lady."

The Battle of Mystria

Before Kaito and Liv could leave for their journey back to The Kaito Harayuma

Empire, two cloaked men walked into Liv and Kaito's room.

"You must come with us. It is not safe here anymore," said one of the cloaked men with a solemn tone in his voice.

Kaito grabbed his sword from the edge of the room and put on his armor. As he and the two cloaked men walked out of the room, fire erupted from the outer village, and the sounds of children and noblemen screaming filled the inside of the town with fear. Kaito and Liv ran through the village following the two cloaked men.

"You must go down this tunnel. It will not be long before they breach the walls," said the other cloaked man as he drew his sword and ran towards the walls.

"Guess we have no choice but to listen," said Kaito as he hustled down the stairs into the deep underground tunnel. The door shut behind them, leaving them with only the light of the dimly lit candles. The tunnel was long and damp, but after a while, it came to an opening.

What Kaito and Liv saw amazed them. It was a massive underground chapel.

And at the altar was a priest. On the stairs of the altar was Queen Saga praying to her god.

"Thronos, please give me the power and strength to defeat my enemies," Queen Saga said in an angered tone. When she got up, she turned around. "We must fight. Or else all my people will die, my kingdom will fall."

Queen Saga grabbed onto the armor that Kaito was wearing. Above them, the Eldandoorian army attacked. At the front of this attack was the young king Dracous, whom nearly every man in every kingdom feared. He was known for being even madder than his father, and he was the one who enslaved the Harayuma people and kept Princess Liv trapped in the castle.

"This ladder leads out of the city into the front of the outer walls; Mystria will fall without your help."

Queen Saga was enraged, and her eyes began to turn to a purplish hue.

"If we have no chance, we will fight," said Kaito as he ran for the ladder. What he saw when he got to the top amazed him. It was an army with about five thousand men. On top of the walls were the graceful men of

Mystria, but they were not shooting bows. Instead, they grabbed rocks, and as they threw those rocks, fire erupted into the middle of the army. King Dracous caught a glimpse of Liv and raced towards her. Before he could get too close, a fireball came crashing down and inflamed his horse.

"Protect Liv, I will fight," said Kaito to Queen Saga. He pulled out his sword from the sheath and ran directly into the middle of the battle. Three men ran towards him. The first one swung for Kaito's head, but Kaito was quicker. He was able to blow the first strike and hit the man in the hand, cleaving the head straight off. As the man fell to the ground in pain, Kaito swung again, splitting the man's head in half. The second man swung towards Kaito, but Kaito was able to dodge right before it hit him. The other man ran towards Viper's sword, pointed it, and tried to stab Kaito in the chest. Kaito blocked the attack, knocking the man to the ground and his sword flying. Kaito's sword goes directly through his heart, and the other man gets a flaming rock to the chest. A group of the army with about twenty soldiers comes screaming towards Kaito. An allied horse comes rushing towards the group with a flaming morning star. He kills all the men within seconds.

A man comes from behind Kaito, catching him off guard. The man is painted in blood, his armor is a crimson red, and his weapon of choice is a two-handed hammer. He swings the hammer with ease and swipes Kaito's legs out, leaving him on the ground. Suddenly, out of nowhere, an arrow comes flying by and hits the man directly in the head, killing him on the spot. Kaito looked over toward the direction of the shot and saw Liv. Liv gave an excited nod and grabbed another arrow. After an hour on the battlefield, Eldandoor's army fled.

"Men fall back. Rest assured, We will be back, not only for Mystria but for Huryama's Empire," said King Dracous as he and his men rode back to Eldandoor. Back in the castle of Mystria, Liv, Kaito, and Queen Saga sat around the meeting table.

"Go back to your people, thanks to your service. We shall live to see another day, and we send men, resources, and extra food your way."

"Thank you, my grace," said Kaito as he bowed and walked away from the queen.

Dragons Rest

Dragons Rest had the largest population in all of Nastomar. It is north of

The Sea of the Dragon and has a population of 1.4 million people. The reason it has such a large population is due to the area of land the kingdom was built on. It was built on a large mountain rich with minerals such as iron, copper, and Figirium. Figirium is one of the weakest materials. Still, when matched well with a piece of steel armor or a weapon, it makes it nearly impenetrable.

"I'll take a loaf of bread," says Prince Bjarne Raeder, first of his name, son of RenFred Raeder. Prince Bjarne was a noble prince. When he wasn't on the battlefield serving as the war commander for his king, he was helping the poor, visiting the chapel of Thornos, and training young men in the way of the sword.

"Thank you, my fair prince. This money will help my family tremendously," the nobleman said as he bowed.

"You are very welcome, kind sir. Keep up the good work," Prince Bjarne said as he walked away. Every morning, Prince Bjarne paid a visit to the merchants. He took in the sights of the city, the grand castle sitting on top of the mountain, the great library where most of the world history sat, and the mess hall where every man and woman could go and eat dinner together in harmony. Prince Bjarne made his rounds and made it back to the castle's throne room, where King Raeder sat.

"You wanted to see me, father?" asked Prince Bjarne.

"Yes, son, the Eldandoorian people have raised an attack on Mystria. A quarter of the Eldandoorian empire was slain in battle, and we have word the Harayuma bloodline is not dead." King Raeder had a very concerned look on his face. He was afraid of what was to come.

"And who is your source of this information about the Harayuma bloodline?" asked Prince Bjarne, questioning the source.

"Lady Vigdis and Lord Torlief have sent word that Kaito Harayuma, the son of Halvard Harayuma, the greatest blacksmith in the four empires, has started a new kingdom. They know this because they were captured on their retreat to our companions in Eldandoor." King Raeder knew the information was true, and he knew if Kaito found out that Dragons Rest was behind the attacks, the four kingdoms would fall as they knew it.

"Father, this could not be true. If this were true, hundreds, if not thousands, of men would be dead. The Harayuma are too much of a threat to be left alive. If Kaito were to find out that you were the one behind the attack, we would all die. It would be the end of the world." Prince Bjarne was in utter fear and shock.

"It's not all bad. Lady Vigdis and Lord Torlief have infiltrated the kingdom. They are allowing Kaito to build his kingdom, but when the time is perfect, we will sail across the Sea and kill them all, every man, woman, and child that seeks the Reign of the Harayuma." King Raeder had already been scheming for this very situation. They knew what threat the Harayuma family was; they might seem like a noble family, but it was quite the opposite. The last time a Harayuma reigned over the kingdoms, hell was set free, and the undead armies came and wiped out about half of the population of the world. If they allowed Kaito to take reign again, they could only imagine what would happen to the four kingdoms.

"I know what we must do, we must hire the twins," said King Raeder.

The Forgotten City

The Forgotten City is the longest-standing kingdom built in the middle of the burning desert. It is ruled by a very young and power-hungry king, who is said to be the most violent in all of Nastomar. He has two daughters named Murieall Duaeni, first of her name, and Tully Duaeni, first of her name. They are known all around Nastomar for owning and operating one of the most prominent mercenary bands and for being world-renowned assassins. If someone wants you dead and has enough gold, you will be dead.

The Ladies were hundreds of miles away from the central city, and they were training to raid and take back a tiny town of rebels outside of The Forgotten City. King Duaeni was ruthless when it came to rebels. If anyone rebels against The Forgotten City, they are killed in combat or thrown in the sandy keep underneath The Forgotten City. The twin sisters rode side by side while an army of 700 mercenaries marched behind them. The band of mercenaries wasn't your ordinary mercenaries, though. They were worse. Over half of the band wore Figirum steel armor, which is practically impenetrable and super heavy. Most of the men also used two-handed weapons made of Figirium steel. The other half of the band would use longbows with firing arrows; they would shoot so many that it would create a massive barrage in the sky, and as it rained down, it created fire everywhere they touched.

When the twins made it to the tiny town of rebels, they realized something odd: it seemed abandoned. "That's strange. We had a man on the inside say that they were here yesterday," said Tully, confused, looking around the home. Out of nowhere, the screams of the rebels were heard. They had attempted to flank and surprise the mercenary band, but they were unsuccessful. Three hundred and sixty-seven of the rebels were killed and hung from the walls of The Forgotten City. It was a grim sight; the men were gutted, and their intestines were what hung them from the wall. The women were kept and sold to brothels to be used as prostitutes. And the children were taken in by the twins to be used as the following line of mercenaries. Twenty mercenaries died on the battlefield, but there were sixty-four children from the ages of ten to sixteen to replace the dead mercenaries.

Murieall and Tully went to the throne room to meet with their father because he had big news. "You wanted to see us, father?" asked Murieall as she bent her knee in front of her father. Tully did the same shortly after.

"Yes, my children, we have disturbing news. Word has it, the Harayuma bloodline is not gone forever. In fact, it is quite the opposite. He has gained Mystria's trust." The king was not scared but excited. This meant he got to show off his power and potentially kill the last Harayuma alive.

"And what about our people across the seas? Can they help?" asked Tully. King Duaeni had previously sent men to assist Eldandoor in conquering Mystria.

"The battle of Mystria was a hard-fought battle, but most of our men have been lost. King Raeder expects a visit from you two shortly. You must sail to Dragons Rest, just the two of you, and find out what he is planning. Afterward, you are to go to the mainland and assist in the war on

Mystria. We will not fail again." King Duaeni spoke sternly, instilling fear into his children.

"Yes, Father, we will not fail again," said Murieall as she stood herself up and bowed to her father.

As the twin sisters walked out of the throne room, Tully said, "I want to be the one to kill that wicked bitch Queen Saga."

"Well, then I'll be the one to behead the last Harayuma," said Murieall. They both chuckled to themselves as they walked to the docks at the end of the city. A long journey was in front of them, one that would make a grown man cry out of fear.

The Devil's Bandits

The Devil's Bandits were one of the most chaos-inducing. They were a group of the five most powerful assassins in all of Nastomar. Lucky for them, they knew who the true king of Nastomar was supposed to be, and it wasn't any of them, but most definitely Kaito Harayuma. Currently, they were marching through the small town of WintersCrest, a few miles east of the dead city. The town of WintersCrest was the Devil's Bandits hideout. Most of the people there either feared them and hated them or loved and worshiped them.

The Devil's Bandits consist of Cenric Hayes, a tall, bulky man in his twenties who wields a large Figiruim steel warhammer, his younger brother Holden Hayes who was only sixteen, has an elven-made longbow from before the first reign of men, Kenelm Randem was a bastard of the Chadwicke family, which made him kill his father and wicked sister. He wields a morning star made of dark steel that he stole from a Harayuma forge years back. Algar Forde is a tall man who wears no armor at all and has the nickname "unhittable" because he is so swift with his spear that nobody has laid a blow on him before. And finally, the leader of the devil's bandits, Oswald Edgare, his name means "God." Some say he is immortal because no matter how hard he gets hit on the battlefield, he never dies. He wields a war axe made of lightbar steel, a scarce steel only forged by the dwarven people who used to live under Mystria.

"Look, men, we have a serious task at hand, and we must protect the Harayuma bloodline at all costs. I have word that the Eldandoor will be knocking on The Kaito Harayuma Empire door shortly. We are going to be their saviors. We cannot let The Kaito Harayuma Empire be wiped from existence." Oswald says this as he knocks back a drink of cheap wine from the tavern in WintersCrest. It's a tiny and cramped tavern, but they make it work for their meetings.

"I have sent word to The Kaito Harayuma Empire that we will be joining them in battle, and King Kaito expects us soon so that we will set out for the kingdom at dusk. We cannot be caught on our journey, or we will most likely be faced with a blood bath." Cenric says as he is polishing the front end of his war hammer. The men sat around the table as the sun began to set.

"Here's our plan: we journey west towards the dead city. Since it's night, the odds of us being attacked are slim," said Kenhelm, the smartest member of the Devil's Bandits. "If we leave now, we will be at The Harayuma gates by daylight." They all get up from the table and put their weapons in their respectable places. Before they hopped on their horses, Oswald gathered them in a circle and said, "Men, this could very well be our last outing as a team. I have a feeling the war against Eldandoor will be a bloody and cold one."

They hopped on their horses and began to ride in total darkness, with only the light of a single torch to lead them. As they left WintersCrest, they spoke of the war to come and how easily this could become the end of the world, with the blood of everyone in the hands of one empire. They knew the Devil's Bandits were the only way that The Kaito Harayuma Empire and bloodline would be secured, and if they didn't fight their hardest for their one true king, they would die alongside him.

As they rode towards The Kaito Harayuma Empire, they spotted a scouting party with the Eldandoorian flag raised. "Men, this is our first test. Leave one of them alive to send a message to Eldandoor; the rest of them are marked for death. Now ride into battle and win," Oswald says. The five men ride into battle, hopping off their horses as they get close to the men. There were at most eighteen men armed to the teeth with weapons. The men of Eldandoor didn't know what hit them. Before they knew it, there were five armed killers among them, eager and prepared to kill.

Cenric pulled his war hammer to the side and swung, swiping one of the men off his feet. As he picked up the hammer, another one of the men screamed and rushed towards Cenric, only to be shot by his brother Holden. The first man, still writhing in pain on the ground, screams out, "For the love of the gods, don't kill me!"

"For the king of Nastomar, you must die." Cenric says as he smashes the man's head underneath the head of the

Warhammer. On the other side of the battlefield were Oswald, Kenelm, and Algar, surrounded by men who were so naive to the absolute horrors those three men were. Oswald reared back for his strongest attack. As he swung his war axe, he split three of the men straight through the middle, leaving their bodies in halves on the ground, bleeding.

Behind Oswald stood Algar, spinning his spear steadily and speedily. Two of the men rushed towards Algar, but Algar dodged both of their attacks with sheer precision, stabbing through the head. The tip of the spear came out through his eye socket. As he pulled the spear out of his face, the eyeball was still stuck on the spear, and the other man stood beside him in fear. Algar was smart about this man. He swiped his legs out from beneath him.

"As far as you are concerned, all your men are dead; run home and tell your king the Devil's Bandits fight under Harayuma. If we catch you on the battlefield again, you will be killed mercilessly."

The last eleven men spread across the battlefield with no lights left suddenly saw a tiny spark of fire flare from the distance as it slowly grew near a fiery steel bad smashed in their face, one by one the last eleven men fell to Kenelm's morning star, they all attempted to run, but Kenelm caught up with them no matter how fast they ran.

The five men stood right in view of The Kaito Harayuma Empire's wall, and the kingdom had already grown into a nice fortified village. "This is it, men. How about we go visit our king." Oswald says as he wipes away the Eldandoorian men's blood from his face.

The Kaito Harayuma Empire

The same night The Devil's Bandits fought the Eldandoorian scouts, King Kaito and Lady Liv entered the walls of the kingdom for the first time after the city's makeover. Lady Vigdis and Lord Torlief both stood right inside the walls, waiting for their return.

"My Lord, my Lady, if we may have a word with you," said Lady Vigdis.

"What is it, Lady Vigdis?" asked Kaito. Although he seemed annoyed, he already knew what she would say.

"You have six people who would like to see you, five members of an organization named the Devil's Bandits, and one girl who I believe would become very valuable to your team." Lord Torlief says as they walk towards the war table.

As they stood around the table, King Kaito said, "What are you waiting for? Send the girl in. I'm eager to meet her, and I would like to do so alone, just Lady Liv and I."

"As you wish, my grace," said Lady Vigdis as she bowed and walked out of the room with Lord Torlief.

Aislinn walked in. She was young but beautiful, she had shorter dark hair, and she had an eager demeanor.

"Your grace, my Lady," she says as she bows. "I am Aislinn. I sailed from Frost Fall to meet you. I am sure Lady Vigdis has filled you in at least a little bit. I have acquired a pair of weapons like no other, but I have a pair of Emberite daggers. Not only that, but I am trained in silent killing. I know I am young, but I must ask that you let me fight with you in this upcoming war."

"So you came from Frost Fall just to meet a king? Yes, you are quite young for a warrior, but we need all the help we can get, so I guess you can fight for us, just don't die. Your weapons are too valuable to be lost to the Eldandoorian scum." King Kaito said this, and Lady Liv agreed with him all the way. She knew this was the only way we could win, with what little help they could get.

"Now run along, Aislinn. I have more people to meet." Lady Liv said, shooing the girl away because she was eager to meet the Devil's Bandits.

As Aislinn left, the five members of the Devil's Bandits walked in. They had not only the aura of urgency but the aura of power, almost as if they could quickly kill King Kaito if they wanted to. Oswald, the leader of the Devil's Bandits, was the one who spoke on behalf of all of the men.

"My grace, My Lady. As you know, we are the Devil's Bandits. My men and I are your strongest allies in this battle. We not only know the enemy, but we believe in you. You are our true king, the true king of Nastomar, and we will battle alongside you until our deaths. We have already stopped a scouting party from entering your walls. I give it another day before their whole army is at your doorstep."

"As you know, we are but a small empire. We don't have the power to overthrow a whole army alone, we have no backers in this battle, Mystria is too weak to fight, and we were unable to get word to any king or queen anywhere north of the sea, so we are alone and weak, we are fighting a losing battle, but just as my mother taught me, that doesn't mean we shall back down. We will not lose this battle, and I will reign supreme over all the kingdoms of Nastomar." King Kaito had not gone mad, but he was determined to win, and he would not quit until he found who was responsible for the purge of his family.

As soon as the conversation between King Kaito and the Devil's Bandits ended, the horns sounded, and the first group of the Eldandoorian army was on their doorstep. This was way earlier than expected. Kaito stood on top of the wall, staring at the number of enemies in front of him.

"How many fighting men do we have?" asked King Kaito.

"About four hundred and sixty," said Lord Torlief.

"And how many do we believe are out there?"

"About seven or eight hundred men." Lord Torlief said again, having a sense of anger in his voice, "And is the king in the mix of these men?"

"No, Your Grace, he has not made his presence known. This wasn't supposed to happen so soon. There are too many of them, and we must wave the flag and give up." Lord Torlief said, giving his first piece of advice to King Kaito.

"We do not give up in the face of our enemies, and I will shatter the skulls of every one of these men and send them back to the gates of Eldandoor." King Kaito said, gripping the grip of his darksteel sword.

Frost Fall

It has been about a week since Aislinn left for The Kaito Harayuma Empire. Search efforts for the girl are still going strong. The kingdom of Frost Fall is not necessarily small, but it isn't that large, either. It is mainly used as a fishing kingdom, although there are some farming families, such as the Aislinns and the Willdarde family, who loved their daughter very much and were willing to go to any lengths to find her.

A raven flew into the port of Frost Fall carrying a letter directed to Aislinn's mother, Daisy. It read:

"Hello, Mom. I know you are probably concerned about my disappearance, and I just want to say I am very sorry for leaving without warning, but I am safe for the most part. The Eldandoorian's first command rank army is at the gates of The Kaito Harayuma Empire, preparing to attack. I will be fighting on the frontlines for the one true king, Kaito Harayuma, but this battle might already be a lost cause. I am writing to you to ask for your help. Please, ask King Irwine to send some of his men to our empire. If we do not get any help, we will be killed within days. Tell Father, I am sorry for what I have done to our family, but it is for the better. Love your daughter, Aislinn."

Daisy was glad to hear from her daughter for the first time in a week but was fearful of the fact that she was fighting on the front lines.

"Honey, I must go to the king. I have some business to attend to," she said to her husband, Clive.

As the day went on, she got farther and farther into the kingdom. The massive mountainous castle drew closer and closer, and by nightfall, she had reached the castle and was stopped by the guards.

"Ma'am, on what business are you attempting to enter the castle?" asked the guard who was in front of the door to the castle.

"It's my daughter, sir, Aislinn. I have gotten word from her that she is caught in the crossfire of a war in the south. She asks me to get as many men as possible to back up their kingdom." Daisy was typically a charismatic person, but she had tears rolling down her face and was growing more and more overwhelmed by the situation by the second.

"Go right ahead to the throne room, my Lady. I'm sure the king will be happy to see you," said the guard.

As Daisy entered the castle, she saw the size of the king's guards. They were giants at least six feet tall and wearing full steel armor. Daisy walked into the throne room, and the king sat on a massive throne made of steel forged by the Harayuma family thousands of years ago.

"Your grace, I come with a severe matter. My daughter, Aislinn, is trapped in the middle of one of the largest wars Nastomar has ever seen. She is fighting on the front lines against Eldandoor. She fights for the last remaining Harayuma. King Harayuma asks for your help in this matter. Without your support, thousands will die, my daughter will die, and my daughter is on the losing side, but I am very certain that if you send troops, your grace, we will win this war. We will be backing one of the most powerful empires ever to be born," Daisy spoke erratically, not giving any room for breath between her words.

"I trust you, Daisy, and I trust your judgment on the matter. I will send six hundred of my best soldiers to fight in this battle, but if we lose, this will be on you," said the king as he looked to his war commander and gave a nod.

"Thank you, your grace. This will not be forgotten, and I will forever be in your court," Daisy said as she bowed to the king.

Dragons Rest

The ship holding the Duaeni twins had finally made it to the kingdom of Dragons Rest. Prince Bjarne met the twins at the docks.

"My ladies, I am sure you know what the king has called you here for, and I hope you are eager for this opportunity," Prince Bjarne said as he walked the twins to the castle, showing them the main streets of the town. As they walked towards the throne room, every single king's servant bowed at the twins and the prince.

"Oh yes, the twins of The Forgotten City, I have heard so much about you," said King Raeder. "As you know, the Harayuma bloodline was not wiped entirely. One of the little cancerous rats escaped. I will pay a great sum of gold and weapons to your people if you can bring me the heads of both King Kaito and Lady Liv. We shall strike immediately, wiping the Harayuma scum from the boots that we so valiantly wear. I ask one thing of you twins: you sail to the south immediately and rescue one key person from their kingdom, Randel. He has many secrets for us to be told, and we must ensure his safety."

King Raeder had been planning this since he got word from Eldandoor that they would be causing a great war on The Kaito Harayuma Empire. King Raeder knew what was at stake if he allowed Kaito to win this war. If he won, the world could easily fall, and everyone would lose everything that they worked for.

"Your grace, what will happen if we fail? Are the rumors of the Desolation true? Will this truly cause the world to end as we know it?" Tully asked. Tully was never the intelligent twin. Some would say she was a sheep. She followed and agreed with everything she believed in, and it weighed her down.

"Although we have no proof that the desolation will be among us again, we must lower the chances of it happening. We know what Kaito wants. He already has one of his puzzle pieces, a pawn in his game. If we allow him to win this battle and let Eldandoor fall, not only do we lose one of our greatest allies and our one chance to take Nastomar, but we will lose our way into the south. He already has Mystira on his side, and if he takes control of Eldandoor, he could very well close the docks to all outsiders. We would have no opportunity to eliminate our enemy. There is no greater time than now; if he falls now, we will win, we will be the victorious party, and we will rule Nastomar."

King Raeder stands up from his throne, holding a goblet of wine in his hands, "For the sake of Nastomar, we must win!"

Screamed out the Duaeni twins, holding their goblets high above their heads.

"You set out tomorrow; you take all of your men from The Forgotten City, and we will send all of our men as well. He has no powerful allies; we will put his empire in a chokehold, strangling his empire of all resources and power. Prince Bjarne and I must stay in Dragons Rest to keep the peace among our people. But rest assured, we back this cause one hundred percent."

King Raeder knew how much power he held in his hands, and he had the most potent and intelligent son. If he were lost on the battlefield, the kingdom of Dragons Rest's power would drop dramatically. And if he lost his only son, he would most definitely go mad, and there is an unlimited length that a father would go for his son. Nor is there a length a king would go to protect his people. A true king would do anything to protect his realm, even if some would call him mad. King Raeder knew what was at stake. Even if sending all of his men was a significant risk, he was willing to gamble it all away at the chance to save Nastomar. The Kaito Harayuma Empire cannot prevail.

The Kaito Harayuma Empire

The Eldandoorian Army stood still in the dark of night, waiting to draw out the army of The Kaito Harayuma Empire.

"Your grace, what shall we do?" asked Oswald, staring intently at the number of torches that lit up the battlefield below them.

"There is only one thing to do: we fight." Kaito stood in front of his men, only the light of a torch shining onto his face, and even then, the fire in his eyes burned bright. "Men, it is all or nothing. Now is the time we reign victorious over our oppressors; now is the time we lay our lives down for Nastomar. Now is the time you lay your life down at the feet of the king. We will not lose. We may be a small empire. Still, if we win this war, we will take all of the South. I will be the king of the south, and you will be my people, so go, fight for the good of Nastomar. Fight for your king!"

Kaito Harayuma learned a great number of lessons from his father, not only in the trade of blacksmithing but also in the skill of charisma and how to lead men into a battle that not a single one of them thought they could win. Kaito knew it was all or nothing.

"Open the gates, follow the lead of me and the Devil's Bandits. The rest of you must follow our lead or die trying!" The wind from standing on the wall blew the fire of the torch all over. It made Kaito's cheeks rosy and cold. As the gates opened, Kaito led the charge, unsheathing ShadowBlade from its sheath. "ATTACK!" screamed Kaito as he charged head-first into the hundreds of armed forces in front of him.

Oswald and his men were directly behind Kaito, keeping him protected from behind. As he ran closer and closer to the center of the battlefield, opposing forces ran towards him. His first opponent was a tall man holding a two-handed sword, but right away, Kaito noticed his weakness. His stance was weak and widespread. Kaito saw this as the perfect opportunity to strike. As the opponent's sword flung forward, Kaito dodged with great speed, putting more distance between himself and the blade of his sword. With one fell swoop of Kaito's

DarkSteel sword, he pierced the opponent's chest plate, leaving him vulnerable. The opponent's sword was stuck in the ground, and the darkness made it hard to see Kaito, as in this war, he wore the brand-new armor he had smithed himself. It was matte black, and the helm covered nearly his whole face, leaving just enough space for Kaito to see. Kaito drew his sword back, and the fight quickly ended for the man in front of him as Kaito stabbed him right through the hole in his chest plate.

Oswald and the rest of the Devil's Bandits were in deep enemy territory, surrounded by men on every side. Cenric was smart about his placement in the enemy territory, being surrounded by men with heavy weapons and armor. Still, there was one major flaw in the Eldandoorian armor: their helmets were made quickly and were weak to heavy blows. All Cenric had to do was aim for the head and hit first, and he would be victorious. Three heavy brutes clobbered close to Cenric, too close for their health, and quickly, it ended one by one as Cenric aimed for head after head. One swung towards Cenric with a great axe, and

Cenric ducked the swing, peeking up in the man's face.

"Peek a boo," Cenric said right before he stabbed the man in the eye with the pointy tip at the bottom of his hammer. Blood splattered everywhere as Cenric pulled the tip out of the man's face. It blinded another man beside him. Cenric knew he could easily take the man out, so he swung with all of his strength, smashing the man's head. The sound of the soldier's skull being crushed filled Cenric with the utmost enjoyment of every enemy he killed. He could feel himself becoming more and more powerful and had more bloodlust.

Meanwhile, at the far back of the Eldandoorian Army stood Aislinn with her new shiny weapons. The men in the back were still too far away from the walls to see that the battle had truly started, yet another flaw in the war commander's plan. Aislinn stood behind the enemy lines, slowly creeping towards the men. She called this tactic "Creeping Death." As soon as one man heard the crunching of leaves, he walked off. Aislinn lured the man towards the thick forest not too far away from the man; she hid behind a tree, and as soon as the man walked close enough, she grabbed onto the man's neck and slit his throat, cutting straight through. The man attempted to scream but instead gurgled on his blood, choking on the blood that pooled up in his mouth.

On the other side of the battlefield, Kenelm was split from the rest of the men. Three men ran up to Kenelm. Kenelm was the most inexperienced fighter from the Devil's Bandits, although he was a great fighter. Kenelm saw the men running towards him, and he immediately began to spin his morning star around. One man got close, and as Kenelm swung the morning star towards him, the man moved out of the way, and the soldier left enough room between Kenelm and himself so he could still hit Kenelm with his sword but could not be hit by the small morning star. The man swung his sword and kicked Kenelm in the arm, only scratching the first layer of armor he was wearing.

"You fool, now you must die." Kenelm said with a cheeky grin on his face before he swung the morning star, which smashed through the man's chest, leaving holes almost like Swiss cheese in his chest. "Puny weaklings the lot of you are. If the rest of you dare charge me, you will seal your fate just like your friend." Kenelm struck fear into the other two men who opposed him. Consequently, they dropped their weapons.

"You seriously thought I would spare your lives?" Kenelm said, chuckling loudly. He swung his morning star, crushing one of the men's skulls, and the other man began to run, only to be shot by a stray arrow seconds later.

Inside The Harayuma Walls

Inside the Empire walls, Lady Liv stood at the war table planning the counterattack on the Eldandoorian Kingdom. Lady Liv stood around the table with Holden and Algar from the Devil's Bandits. Alongside her were Lady Vigdis and Queen Saga, who were able to bring together an army from nearly every town and city in the southern Isles.

"My Lady, if we sneak out the back gates of the kingdom, we could sneak through the forest and make a surprise attack on Eldandoor. Over half of the king's army is here, at our walls. If we attack them with all of our troops, we might be able to overpower them quickly without much of a threat, and the only danger is the king guild. Eldandoor has a guild of skilled fighters that are always by his side no matter what." Queen Saga says while moving pawns around on the map on the table.

"How many are in the king guild?" asked Lady Liv while tapping her fingers across the side of the table.

"Last time, I was told, about five or ten of them, all skilled in the art of swords." Queen Saga knew this information due to the alliance she used to have with King Viper before she chose to side with Kaito.

"It's about a two-day journey, and if we travel throughout day and night, it might be a whole day journey," Algar said, already having experience with long travels from kingdom to kingdom.

"I say we can take Eldandoor within three days if we play our cards right. If the king falls, we will have secured nearly half of Nastomar." Holden says with a look of resolution in his eyes, "we send half our forces now. We start digging trenches and building a siege party. The other half can back up the front lines and help get Eldandoor off our backs." Lady Liv says with a tone of dire importance in her voice.

She has learned to become a very persistent and intelligent Lady. After all, she wants to serve the one true king of Nastomar. She has to learn and adapt to his ways quickly. "I know Eldandoor, the king will not leave his chambers unless drawn out by the thought of regaining the princess. I will be the one to kill the king when the time comes."

Lady Liv hated the man she was supposed to marry, and the king was a very wretched and violent person; in fact, Lady Liv calls him the devil of Nastomar. "If Kaito would want anyone to lead the attack on foreign land, he would choose me." Lady Liv knew what Kaito wanted. After all, that was her one true love. She had never had such a love as the love she had for him.

The Battlefield

Out on the battlefield sat the corpses of almost three hundred men from both sides. Kaito, Aislinn, Oswald, Cenric, and Kenelm all stood at different locations on the battlefield. The break of dawn had just come, leaving the Harayuma more defenseless due to their armor and weapons being camouflaged in the darkness. Kaito stood on a mound of bodies of both courageous comrades and the scum that killed them. Suddenly, the gates of the empire opened. Six hundred new allies marched through those gates, and for the first time, Kaito's chances of victory were looking up; he may have had a chance of victory.

"Kaito, your grace, Lady Liv and Queen Saga seek a word with you." A valiant ally said to Kaito as he hopped off his horse, "Take my horse. It's much safer than running." Kaito hopped on the stallion and rode towards the walls. As he entered, he saw Lady Liv, Lord Vigdis, Lord Torlief, Algar, Holden, and Queen Saga standing at the gates waiting for him. "I have made plans to flank our enemy on their land, and we will be marching to Eldandoor now. We have sent more troops to back your battle on the front lines." Lady Liv gave Kaito her first real kiss on the lips before walking towards the back gates. "Your grace, don't die out there. We're counting on you," Algar said as he took his arm off Kaito's shoulder.

Meanwhile, Aislinn was still at the back of the battlefield, cutting her way through the enemies. Overnight, she killed one hundred and sixty-seven of the three hundred and forty-eight men who died. Within an hour after the party led by Lady Liv left, the battle had been won. Every enemy who was not killed in combat was either taken hostage or fled back home. Aislinn and the rest of the army met in the middle of the war-torn battlefield. "My warriors, you fought courageously. We only won due to the efforts of Queen Saga. Those of you who made it through the battle, go back to the kingdom. Wash up and prepare for the next battle. I have gotten word that Dragons Rest and The Forgotten City are both going to attack soon. We have about four days to prepare. For those who want to help prepare, go with Oswald. He will tell you what must be done."

Kaito was slowly shaping into the true king of Nastomar; he was learning the art of battle, the way a king should treat his followers, and the ins and outs of romance. Kaito hasn't forgotten what lies ahead and what is at stake, not only the lives of his people but the lives of his bloodline. If he loses this war, his bloodline will be dead forever, and it will be nonexistent. He will have failed what his mother and father died for. Kaito went back to the battlefield to help Oswald prepare for the largest battle in the history of Nastomar. "How many will be knocking at our gates?" asked Kaito. "Roughly a million. The odds of us surviving this battle are a million to one. A real miracle would have to happen for us to win alone," Oswald said as he dug a section of the trench on the beach where the enemy ships would be docking.

"And if we take over Eldandoor? How many will fight for us?" asked Kaito as he crunched the numbers in his head, preparing for what was to come. "We would have roughly four hundred and sixty thousand between Eldandoor, our kingdom, the remainder of the people in Ember Fall and Mystria, and the surrounding cities and towns," Oswald said, still digging the trench. "Now, why don't you grab a shovel and get to work," Oswald said sarcastically.

"How about Frost Fall? What's their take on this?" asked Kaito as he picked up a shovel and began to dig alongside Oswald. "If they join our cause, we will have won. The people of Frost Fall are strong, and if they are fighting for something they know is for the greater good, we will win," Oswald said. "But the odds of them getting involved are slim?" asked Kaito. "They have never actually fought in a war anywhere other than their land," said Oswald.

Aislinn walked up behind Kaito. "Your grace, may I have a word in private?" "You may," said Kaito as he walked away from the trench with Aislinn. "What is it, my Lady?" asked Kaito with a concerned look on her face. "Frost Fall backs you. We will win this battle. You will be the true king of Nastomar," Aislinn said, holding onto Kaito's shoulder pads. "They will be here before nightfall, their entire army at your hands.

Eldandoor

Two days after the victory on the homefront, the battlefield was prepped and ready for the battle at Eldandoorian gates.

"Men, ladies, warriors, today we storm the kingdom of Eldandoor. We do not stop until every man, woman, and child quakes at our feet. The goal is not to kill everyone but instead to take the kingdom for our cause, and we need this more now than ever. If we fail this mission, every single one of us will die for nothing, for a cause that means nothing. Remember, you are not alone in this battle. You may die alone but live in a world among men. Fight with your all, give it your whole. Not for me, not for you, but for Nastomar. The Eldandoorian scum want us all dead, all because of our king, the one true king of Nastomar. We will not let the scum and the enemies of the world take our king from us! March forth and storm the castle!"

Lady Liv was becoming the most powerful lady in all of Nastomar; she was the only princess ever to stand up to her house and rebel against her own family. Lady Liv rode towards the gate.

"Let me in or pay the consequences!" Lady Liv shouted to the man who stood above the gate. He was very anxious at the presence of the army and the manpower, but most importantly, Lady Liv had a dark flame glowing in her eyes. She would torch her own home if it meant Kaito would rule; she stood on the same drawbridge that her father was shot on, and the bloodstain was still there.

"We cannot let you in. You will have to kill us all before we allow you to enter our home!" said the guard. His voice was trembling. He knew if he said another word, a crossbow bolt would be fired directly into his face.

"If you shall not let us pass, we will burn your kingdom to the ground, and it will no longer stand after I and my warriors are finished."

Lady Liv gave Algar the signal to begin the barrage on the walls.

"Load your bows… Hold… Fire."

Algar had just given the word to let a large barrage of arrows fly into the kingdom of Eldandoor. Men fell off the walls like boulders rolling down a mountain. The hill-like terrain made the perfect cover for the archers fighting under Lady Liv. After two hundred men and three hours passed, the foot soldiers put their ladders up against the walls and began jumping over the walls. One by one, the foot soldiers began raiding the town, kicking in every door and taking every nobleman, woman, and child hostage. One of the men opened the gates for Lady Liv to enter through. Holden and Algar followed through after a long battle. Algar, Holden, and Lady Liv made it to the castle. A king's guild member stood on top of the stairs into the throne room. He held an emberite spear.

"I'll take this one, my Lady," said Algar as he grabbed the spear off his back and walked to the floor at the top of the stairs.

"So you are the first of our many foes in this castle?" said Algar, circling the king's guild member. He said nothing before he lunged forward and jabbed the once unhittable man in the chest, sending him flying down the stairs. When he hit the bottom of the stairs, his body lay lifeless, just as if his soul had left his body. But Holden put his hand over the wound and said a chant,

"Thornos, Thornos, may my brother in arms rise again to defeat our enemies. Thornos, Thornos."

Within seconds, the wound began to heal. Algar leaped to his feet. This time, he ran up the stairs, and right as the king's guard member's head was in his sight, Algar threw the spear, landing directly in the middle of the man's face, right between the eyes and above the nose.

"God damn, that was the closest I've been to dying," Algar said as he ripped the spear from the lifeless man's corpse that was stapled to the wall. As they walked side by side, the party spoke amongst themselves.

"You said thirty of them, correct?" asked Lady Liv.

"No more than thirty."

As soon as that happened, three more Kings guild members hopped down from the rafters. The one on the right side held two daggers. He was more than short, and he was a dwarf.

"Well, I've never seen a Dwarven assassin," Holden said as he chuckled to himself.

The man in the middle held a longbow, and he had lifeless eyes, almost like he didn't have a soul.

"By the gods, he's a freak!" screamed out Algar, pointing at the man.

On the left was a woman. She was tall with dark hair, and it was Lady Liv's captor, the woman who had kept Lady Liv locked in the keep for months. She was holding the same whip that she had beaten Lady Liv with.

"So we meet again, you wicked woman," said Lady Liv as she pulled the arrow back on her bow, aiming for the leg of the woman. She fired her bow, hitting her in the kneecap.

As soon as the arrow was fired, chaos spread in the room. Each of the king's guild members is a soldier: the dwarf going for Holden, the lifeless man going for Algar. Immediately, the lifeless man lunged for Algar, but he had the brains of a dead man. Algar stuck his spear directly out in front of him. The undead-esque man landed directly on the tip of the spear, and it didn't die. Instead, it started viciously shaking and trying to rip toward Algar.

"What the hell is up with this thing!?" shouted Algar before Holden threw one of his spears into the undead creature's head, causing it to fall limp shortly after.

The dwarf with daggers ran towards Holden with his short, stubbly legs. Even though his legs were short, he was fast. Algar stuck his foot out and tripped the dwarf. Algar immediately began cracking up and cackling like a witch. Holden bent over the dwarf and picked it up.

"Awww, look at you; you're so petite and cute."
Holden began to laugh and almost had himself in tears before the dwarf tried kicking him.

"Alright, that's it, you little shit. We can't let a turd like you run around now, can we?" he said before hugging the dwarf and snapping its neck.

"It broke like a stick. That was almost too easy," said Algar, still cracking up over the dwarf.

"Can we stop laughing and kill this witch who tortured me?" said Lady Liv as she was not only angry at the face of the woman she had to fight but at the fact that two absolute buffoons accompanied her.

"Yes, my Lady," said Algar as he walked behind the enemy and grabbed her arms.

Lady Liv began inching closer and closer to the lady.

"Do you have anything to say for yourself?" asked Lady Liv, still willing to give the woman her life if she apologized.

Instead, she spat in the face of Lady Liv.

"You betrayed your name. You are no better than the scum you are fighting alongside," she said right before Lady Liv grabbed the whip she was beaten with as a child.

"This is what I do to those who oppose me."

Lady Liv wrapped the whip around the woman's neck and slowly leaned back, applying pressure slowly. So much pressure was brought onto the woman's head that her eyes popped out of her face, and all the blood vessels burst before she leaned forward lifeless.

"You boys will suffer the same fate if you betray the king. I'll make sure of it," Lady Liv said as she winked at the two men with a smile on her face that stretched from one ear to the other. "Now, boys, why don't we go kill this king," Lady Liv said eagerly. She had waited for the moment to kill the king for years, and now was the best opportunity. Just on the other side of the door she was facing stood a king who would have to fight for his life, even if, in the end, it was worthless.

The Kaito Harayuma Empire

Back at the coast of The Kaito Harayuma Empire, Kaito stared off into the distant ocean, all of his men in position for battle when an old man grabbed Kaito's shoulder.

"Do you remember me, Kaito?" asked the old man.

"Cassius?" asked Kaito.

"You are very close to your goal, Kaito. Do not let your enemies take the south. Remember what is at stake, my boy, do not hold back. I know you have been holding back. These are the men responsible for your family's death, and they wanted the Harayuma bloodline to burn to ashes and blow away in the wind." Cassius stared into Kaito's eyes. "I have one final piece of advice, your advisors… they must be eliminated." Cassius walks away after he speaks those words, and before Kaito knows it, the old man disappears into a thin column of dark ash.

Kaito looked out onto the ocean. Ships were starting to come into view. Within seconds, the battle horn began to blow.

"Men, this is our time. Kill the men who oppose you. Eliminate your enemies. Become victorious!" Kaito screamed as the warriors of Dragon's Rest began storming the beach, with The Forgotten Cities army close behind.

Kaito stood alongside Oswald.

"We hold the beach until Frost Fall comes to join us. If we hold for that long, it won't matter how many die." Kaito says, looking intently and angrily at the war unfolding in front of them.

"The twins are here." Oswald says with a horrified look on his face.

Kaito looked near where Oswald was looking. There stood the two Duaeni twins slashing through the opposing forces left and right. They stood back to back as Kaito's army swarmed them. For a second, it looked as if the battle was already lost. But out of the blue, the twins disappeared. Kaito ran into the battlefield to back up his fellow men, Oswald, Kenelm, and Cenric, who were huddled in a circle.

"The Devil's Bandits might be split, and this could very well be our last battle, but we will fight for our king until death does us part," said Oswald. Oswald was never fearful of anything whatsoever. But when thousands of enemies are swarming your homes, fear is natural. It fills every man, woman, and child at one point or another.

Aislinn was protecting the inside of the walls from any enemies who wandered too close to the kingdom. She knew the Duaeni twins wanted something from inside the kingdom, but she did not know what. Randel stood at the blacksmithing table, still forging weapons for any soldiers who had survived the last battle but lost their weapons. The twins had climbed the weak point of the empire's wall, leading them directly into the center of the town.

"Remember our mission, Rescue Randel, Kill anyone who stands in our way," Murieall said as she and Tully snuck through the city. It was eerie how quiet the city was. All citizens were told to hide in the rooms underneath their homes, and if anyone got into that room, kill them immediately.

Tully heard talking coming from close to the walls. "If I do recall, that sounds like Randel." Murieall said as she hugged the wall of a nearing home to the blacksmith's hut.

"That girl, something is up with that girl," says Tully. She stares at the girl, but she knows she is powerful. She can tell by the way Aislinn carries herself, the way she is speaking to Randel, and the way she is holding her daggers.

"Let's go, now's the perfect chance, I'll grab him, you distract that girl," says Murieall. Murieall runs directly towards Randel, and Tully follows suit, unsheathing her sword and running directly into the grasp of a giant serpent whose bite force is strong enough to crush a grown man's head.

Aislinn sees Murieall run towards Randel. She instantly draws her daggers, but

Murieall is fast. Murieall grabs Randel, throws him over her shoulder, and begins running for the back gate of the kingdom, the one that they use to transport farmed goods and materials.

"Look, I'm Murieall Dueani, and I'm here to take you home. We are your allies, so you better cooperate." Murieall looks back to see Aislinn and Tully standing close to each other.

"Look, girl, I don't want to kill a kid, so just move out of the way and let us go," says Tully, holding her sword close to her chest, still holding a defensive stance.

"So you are one of the Dueani twins, the most powerful mercenaries in the Realm," Aislinn says, chuckling to herself. "You don't look powerful, and your face is suited for a brothel, not the battlefield." Aislinn says, trying to get a reaction out of Tully.

"Why you bitch, I am Tully Dueani from the Forgotten City, daughter of King Dueani." Tully knew what was to come, but she didn't want to be known for killing a kid. Aislinn lunges forward at Tully, attempting to catch her in her defensive stance. But

Tully quickly swings at Aislinn. Aislinn blocks the swing with her two daggers.

"You're fast for a brat," Tully says. Watching Murieall get further and further from Aislinn. Aislinn grins and steps backward. The lady she sees in front of her is tall but has the face of a whore; she is by no means pretty. Tully swings her sword again, only for a loud clash between the metals to ring out.

"I don't want to kill you kid. Just leave." Tully says, growing more and more irritated by the second. The roar of the battlefield sings out from outside the walls.

"You won't kill me, and you'll be the one to die," Aislinn says with a smile before pulling a throwing knife out from her belt. Aislinn throws the knife into Tully's right shoulder. Tully screams out in pain. Tully rushes forward, but Aislinn is too quick. Aislinn slides between Tully's legs. Aislinn peaks up from behind Tully and stabs her right in the back.

"I am Aislinn, from the kingdom of Frost Fall, and I will never die to a bitch that looks like a donkey." Aislinn whispers into Tully's ear before kicking Tully to the ground. A soft thud is heard as she hits the soft dirt beneath her.

Eldandoor

Lady Liv kicks in the door of the king's quarters. In front of her stood a giant. Standing at eight feet tall, smelling of rotten bodies with the slight smell of blood. Behind the giant of a man stood the king.

"Well, well, well. Suppose it isn't the princess herself. Good luck killing…"

"The Boulder, long-dead warrior, yes, of course," says Lady Liv. Algar and Holden drew their weapons. The rattle of their weapons told Lady Liv that they were afraid. The Boulder grabbed Holden. Holden screamed as his head was beginning to crack and creak.

Little did Boulder know he had one weakness: his helmet had a hole for sight, and Holden had a knife the perfect size to fit that hole. Boulder squealed like a baby as the knife dug deeper and deeper into his eye. The sound of the knife digging through his eye was horrid. The eye began to drip blood around the tip of the knife. Boulder dropped to his knees in pain, and Holden ripped out the knife. Holden took the helmet off of the

Boulder's head and began to stab the top of his head repeatedly. Blood began to splatter all around the room, painting Holden's face crimson red and the walls a dark red.

Lady Liv walked up to the king and said, "Do you have any last words?"

"I never liked you. You were a traitor to your name and home. You deserve to rot in hell," the king said before Lady Liv laid him flat on the ground. The thud of her armor-plated fists hitting the king's skull rung out. Punch after punch, Lady Liv beat the king. He cried out in pain, begging her to stop, but Lady Liv couldn't understand him over the sound of him gurgling on his blood. Even after he died, Lady Liv continued to beat him. Algar and Holden had to pull Lady Liv off of the king. She screamed and demanded to be put down, but Algar and Holden did not listen.

After Lady Liv was pulled off of the king, his face was unrecognizable. His face was covered in blood, and his brains appeared to be popping out of his skull.

"I think we have won," Algar said.

"Our next step is to get the people to side with us," Holden said.

Ember Fall

Ember Fall was Kaito Harayuma's home. Burnt to the ground. Left to ruins and ash, a new group appears. They call themselves "The Phoenix Reclaimers." This group emerged from deep inside the rubble of Ember Fall. They know Kaito Harayuma is alive, and they have one goal in mind: rebuild Ember Fall, which was Kaito's hometown, and help Kaito claim the south. These three teenage girls used one weapon, engineered and created by their father, known as the hand cannon. The hand cannon was still a prototype, but their father built four of them, one for himself and one for each of his daughters. The hand cannon was nearly unnoticeable; it sat in the gloves of the armor, and if you squeezed your pinkie finger to your thumb, it would open up the knuckles of your glove and shoot three small yet mighty steel balls. The three girls' names were Seraphina Firesong, the oldest of the group; Emberlyn Firesong, the middle child, the most intelligent of the group; and Avalon Firesong, the youngest child, who loved creating chaos. The girls had plenty of ammo and were ready to back up Kaito in his war.

"Ladies, we shall start our journey to Kaito's new home now! We ride to The Kaito Harayuma Empire, and we kill every single one of the men who destroyed our home. We have the newest technology in the world. We are undefeatable!" Avalon said as she hopped on top of her matte black horse. It had long fur on its legs and feet, but the rest of its fur was short. Emberlyn got on top of her horse, and it was as white as snow but massive. Its breed was a Percheron. Emberlyn knew this because of the size and coloration of the horse. And Seraphina rode a brown horse with black spots. She had no clue what the breed was. But once they got on top of their horses, they rode towards the kingdom of Harayuma Descent. With one goal in mind: to kill every single one of their opponents. Kaito was a charming young man when the ladies met him last. They could hardly imagine how handsome and courageous he had become since then. They were all eager to meet him and become his loyal servants. The horses galloped gallantly. With each step was another step closer to freedom for the realm of Nastomar. The one true king would reign supreme. He was a caring, courageous, steady-headed, and handsome king.

Sun Crest

Sun Crest was a tropical island off the east coast of The Forgotten City. Nobody visits the island, although most people say they are the most wild people in the Realm, only eating fish and goat meat. They need to find out why they choose to stay on such a small island instead of joining a large kingdom. Some speculate that it has to do with fighting underneath someone they don't know, other than fighting their own battles. But Prince Bjarne was about to find out.

Prince Bjarne walked off his battleship onto a foreign land for the first time in his life. The tribe members and the Lord of the island greeted Prince Bjarne.

"What is it you seek in Sun Crest?" asked Lord Getano.

"I seek your men. We are in the midst of a war against the final standing Harayuma. If you help us fight and kill him, we will pardon you and allow you to live peacefully on the island of Sun Crest," said Prince Bjarne.

"And if we don't fight alongside you?" asked Lord Getano.

"I will burn your tribe to the ground, leaving not a single man, woman, or child standing alive," Prince Bjarne chuckled as he said this, spitting in the Lord's face.

"We will fight alongside you as long as you give us a castle and farmland," said Lord Getano.

"A castle and farmland? Is that all you seek?" asked Prince Bjarne.

"Yes, it is. Now, do we have a deal or not?" asked Lord Getano, sticking his hand out towards Prince Bjarne and waiting for a handshake to seal the deal.

"We will give you ten warships. You sail to the south with all of your men and kill the last Harayuma alive. That is your only job, nothing more, and I might even grant you your city," said Prince Bjarne as he shook his hand.

The Kaito Harayuma Empire

On the front lines sat Kaito Harayuma, Aislinn Willdarde, Oswald Edgare, Cenric Hayes, and Kenelm Random. Fighting for their lives. Watching men fight for their lives.

"Frost Fall is supposed to come today?" asked Kaito.

"By nightfall," said Oswald. "I also have word that Lady Liv has taken Eldandoor. Algar and Holden will be returning within the hour, and a new group will be arriving shortly after."

"New group?" asked Kaito.

"A group of survivors calling themselves the Phoenix Reclaimers, a group of three teenagers from Ember Fall." Oswald almost expected Kaito to be sad that only three hundred-odd people survived Ember Fall.

"The FireSong family?" asked Kaito, looking at Shadowblade and wiping the dried blood from its blade.

"Yes, your grace, did you know them?" asked Oswald.

"Their father was an inventor; my father and I built weapons and parts for his blueprints. He built a hand cannon right before he died," Kaito said, reminiscing on the past.

A man fell at Kaito's feet, begging for forgiveness for attacking his home, but Kaito felt no sympathy for the man. "May Thornos bring you happiness," Kaito said before crushing the man's head beneath his boot.

Eldandoor.

Lady Liv sat on the throne of Eldandoor for the first time in her life. "My servants, I have rescued you from the enemy. The king that ruled before me was an evil rapist and backstabber. Kaito Harayuma is the one true king; any who oppose him, come forward. And those who will fight for him, bend the knee now."

Lady Liv wasn't just a lady at that moment; she let her hot head get the best side of her. About sixty men walked towards the throne. Algar went down the line and stabbed them in the heart, one by one, saying, "May Thornos bring you happiness," before killing each man.

"The rest of you are coming with me back to The Kaito Harayuma Empire. Eldandoor has been defeated," Lady Liv said, chuckling maniacally.

Lady Liv and her loyal subjects made it to The Kaito Harayuma Empire right as the Frost Fall soldiers arrived. And half an hour later, The Phoenix Reclaimers made it.

The Kaito Harayuma Empire

Frost Fall took back the south within two hours of the night. Eldandoor had fallen to the feet of the Harayuma Empire. Lady Liv walked up to Kaito and said, "Your grace, I missed you," and gave him a long, loving kiss on the lips.

"This war is not over. Sun Crest has allied with The Forgotten City, and the Forgotten City brings a few hundred more men as well," Oswald said grimly.

"We have plenty of soldiers, and we will win again," Kaito said, holding onto Lady Liv's hand.
Kaito left Oswald and the Devil's Bandits to catch up in the tavern as they waited for the next strike. Lady Liv and Kaito went to their chambers to speak.

"Kaito, what do you know about the Devil's Bandits?" asked Lady Liv.

"I know they worship and idolize Thornos, the god of destruction and war," said Kaito.

"Kaito… I watched Holden revive Algar after he was stabbed and thrown downstairs…" Lady Liv had a fearful look on her face, almost as if she had just seen a ghost.

"Thornos is the true god of Nastomar. Anyone who follows him is granted something special," Kaito said, trying to cheer up his girlfriend.

After a moment, a light knock hit the door.

"Come in!" Lady Liv declared.

Seraphina FireSong walked in through the door and rushed to Kaito to give him a huge hug.

"Kaito! How have you been?" Seraphina said.

"Well, I have been hanging in there. This never-ending war is driving me crazy," Kaito said.

"It's an honor to meet you, your grace," Seraphina said to Lady Liv.

"Oh, I am not the queen," Lady Liv said in a peaceful tone.

"She isn't queen yet. I plan on having a wedding after the war," Kaito said, looking into Lady Liv's eyes.

"Well, that is news to me, your grace," Lady Liv said, shocked.

"I can tell she is powerful," Seraphina said. "She has won Eldandoor for us. We have taken the largest kingdom in the south."

"That is amazing. I plan to rebuild our home, and when that time comes, I want you to rule over Ember Fall," Seraphina said.

"My king will not have time to rule over yet another kingdom. I say you become Lady of Ember Fall," Lady Liv said with a smile on her face.

"That is a wise choice, Liv. You are now Lady FireSong of Ember Fall," Kaito said, shaking Seraphina's hand. "Now, if you will, I must visit Aislinn," Kaito said before kissing Lady Liv and walking away.

In the dark streets of the Kaito Harayuma Empire, Aislinn was alone by a fire.

"I heard you fought a great battle today, Aislinn," Kaito said, proud of the child he sat next to.

"I killed Tully Dueani. One of the most relentless fighters in Nastomar. And yet she didn't even give the battle her all," Aislinn said, sounding very disappointed.

"Why are you so upset, my child?" Kaito asked.

"I let her sister get away with Randel. And Tully didn't give the fight her all; she didn't want to hurt a child." Aislinn almost began to cry out of irritation.

"Randel wasn't even his first name, and he was the son of King Raeder, sent here to spy and share secrets with Lord Torlief and Lady Vigdis. You did us all a favor by allowing him to get away. I want them to know our strategies because if they do, the battle will be more fun and bloody. Just how we like our battles," Kaito said, wiping the tears away from Aislinn's cheeks. "You did amazing, and you killed the most people out of anyone in this war. For that, I am giving you an official status. You are now my war commander. And I am going to fill you in on a secret."

Kaito said, "Lord Torlief and Lady Vigdis will meet their fates, and Prince Bjarne is going to die at our feet. On my wedding day. And you will be there to watch it," Kaito said, smiling ear to ear.

Dragons Rest

Murieall successfully escaped back to Dragons Rest. She walked into the throne room with a grateful look in her eye.

"Your grace, I bring to you, your son," two soldiers pushed Randel forward.
"Hello, my son. How was your time in the south?" asked King Raeder.

"It was fine, Father," said Randel.

"They treated you well, I hope," King Raeder said.

"They did indeed. I gathered plenty of intel," Randel said.

"Where is your sister, Murieall?" King Raeder asked, concerned about the well-being of his family after this venture.

"She was killed in combat trying to bring your son home to you," Murieall snarled. "You got my daughter killed, and for that, I will make sure you pay."

Murieall stormed out of the throne room, more pissed off than she entered the room. She walked to the docks and got onto the ship with one mission in mind: kill King Raeder.

Meanwhile, in King Raeder's war room, Randel began to spill.

"They have Eldandoor, the remainder of its army. They hold the coastal beaches with Frost Falls army. They have a young girl with Emberite daggers crafted by me. Lady Liv has grown to quite the warrior, and she may become a problem down the road. As for their war plans, they did not plan on leaving the South; they held every kingdom in the South other than the City of the Dead. All the docks have been closed and are heavily fortified other than the dock directly in front of The Kaito Harayuma Empire. That was our only way to attack. They had dug large moats and trenches around the docks, making it hard to storm the kingdom. They were well rounded, between their army size and the land they owned. They also have the Devil's bandits and The Phoenix Reclaimers on their side."

Randel spilled all the information he knew, and it feared the king a lot. He knew what was at stake with what little army they sent with Sun Crest.

"We are fighting a losing battle. The odds we win are slim to none," King Raeder said.

"Send word to Lord Torlief and Lady Vigdis that they must escape immediately," King Raeder said to his master, who ran off to write his letter.

"Now we have caused another issue. Murieall wants you dead. And she won't stop until she gets what she wants," Randel said before walking back to his chamber

The Forgotten City

Murieall sailed home swiftly and went to her father.

"Tully is dead, and I am sending what little troops we have left to Dragons Rest. I am killing the King." Murieall was fuming. She had finally snapped, and she would not stop until she got what she wanted. And what she wanted was King Raeder dead.

Murieall had her three most trusted advisors in her underground war room, strategizing for the battle to come. Maps that smelled like old paper and had a yellowish tint to them were sprawled across the table. Candle lights dimly shined in the war room.

Murieall sat around the table studying the strengths and weaknesses of the land around Dragons Rest. It was a mountainous area. She took books from the library that had spy reports on Dragons Rest and how she could quickly eliminate the soldiers with bow and arrow from on top of the mountain behind the castle.

But a raven came in with a letter for her.

"You are needed on the battlefield with all of your men. The siege on The Kaito Harayuma Empire is beginning soon," signed by Lord Torlief.

The Kaito Harayuma Empire

Sun Crest and the remainder of The Forgotten City's army sailed south, while Dragons Rest's forces were delayed at sea due to a severe storm. Murieall disembarked, only for the ship to be bombarded by a hail of flaming arrows. The southern landscape was steeped in death from the ongoing month-long conflict. The shoreline and waters ran red, strewn with wrecked and stranded ships that provided ample cover for enemy forces.

Aislinn spotted Lord Torlief and Lady Vigdis making a dash for a boat offshore, but Aislinn intercepted them. "If you two want to leave, you'll have to kill me," Aislinn declared, locking eyes with Lady Vigdis. Lord Torlief snarled and drew his sword, swinging with enough force to shatter lesser weapons. But Aislinn's blade was no ordinary weapon; it was forged of Emberite, a rare metal found only once in a thousand blood moons. Aislinn parried Lord Torlief's strike, but heard another sword being unsheathed behind her—it was Kaito.

Thus began a two-on-two battle. Kaito faced off against his former loyal advisor, Lady Vigdis, consumed by rage and bloodlust for her involvement in his parents' deaths. Aislinn, stunned to see the king defending her despite their limited acquaintance, was urged by Kaito to protect Lady Liv, warning of Murieall's approach.

"You two disappoint me. I always knew you'd betray me; you helped destroy my home," Kaito seethed, his eyes burning with intensity. Lady Vigdis taunted him cruelly about his mother's death before lunging forward. A clash of metal rang out as Kaito deflected her strike. "My mother was the only person I loved. I'll kill you for even mentioning her," he vowed, lunging and narrowly missing Lady Vigdis with his counterattack.

Lord Torlief seized Kaito from behind, but Kaito's spiked armor allowed him to retaliate, elbowing Lord Torlief and causing a painful scrape along his rib cage. Lord Torlief released Kaito, inadvertently propelling him towards Lady Vigdis, who impaled herself on the spikes. With a swift motion, Kaito activated a hidden mechanism, launching steel balls that fatally struck Lady Vigdis.

"Now, Lord Torlief, for your punishment, I've decided... I'll dismember you limb by limb," Kaito chuckled manically, retrieving a knife from his belt and seizing Lord Torlief's hand. Despite Lord Torlief's struggles and pleas, Kaito began with the index finger, causing excruciating pain until Lord Torlief passed out, after which Kaito swiftly ended his suffering by slitting his throat.

"You were strong, Lord Torlief. What a shame you couldn't endure longer," Kaito murmured, offering a prayer over the fallen bodies. Meanwhile, Aislinn fought her way through heaps of fallen allies on the frontline, using their bodies as shields against arrows. She reached Lady Liv just as Murieall arrived.

"You... you killed my sister," Murieall accused, driven by fury. "If you come any closer to my future queen, I'll kill you both," Aislinn retorted, her eyes flashing with irritation. Murieall shoved Lady Liv aside, causing her to tumble down a steep hill into enemy territory. Though Lady Liv fought valiantly, soldiers from Sun Crest captured her and placed her on a ship bound for Dragons Rest.

Murieall attacked Aislinn, who swiftly drew her daggers and maneuvered beneath her, slashing Murieall's stomach. As they rose, Algar appeared behind Murieall and fatally impaled her with his spear. Blood spilled from Murieall's mouth as she collapsed, her life extinguished.

"Sorry, kid. Couldn't let you kill them both," Algar remarked to Aislinn with a wink. "Looks like you failed to protect Lady Liv." Algar pointed towards the departing ship. "Damn it. Kaito's going to have my head," Aislinn muttered, rushing towards the vessel. Algar followed her onto an abandoned warship, both disappearing without a word to anyone about their destination.

The Sea of the Dragon

The Dragons Rest Army was still held up on the Sea of the Dragon. The terrible storm had passed, and they were on their way to The Kaito HarayumaEmpire. Suddenly, an unknown ship crashed into the side of the DragonsRest boat.

"Pirate!" screamed out the War commander on the ship. A group of pirates jumped on board the ship. The pirate ship flew the flag of the capybara, showing that they were from Sun Crest.

"These are not pirates!" screamed out a soldier as he was being jumped by multiple "pirates."

"These are soldiers from Sun Crest!" screamed out another soldier. Within seconds, the ship was sunk, and every Dragons Rest soldier had died.

The Sun Crest soldiers got onto another warship and disappeared into the foggy sea. As the War Ship disappeared, the sea began to split. A large creature was emerging from the water. But nobody was there to see it happen.

Dragons Rest

Lady Liv arrived at Dragons Rest and was not even brought to King Raeder. Instead, she was brought to the outskirts of an abandoned town, and one of the men wiped sand away from a trapped door.

"Get in, Lady Olivia," said the mysterious man.

"How do you know my name?" Lady Liv asked, her jaw could have hit the ground if there hadn't been a bone stopping it. As she neared the trap door, the rope they used to tie her hands together was cut. And she was walked into a massive room.

"We are the followers of Cassius, and we know everything there is to know about you. We know how you will marry Kaito Harayuma. And how you will bear his child. How you will become the mother of bears and Dragons. How you will rule the realm alongside Kaito for the rest of eternity only for it to end swiftly yet painfully for you," said the man.

"You have three choices. Choose wisely." a cloth was removed, revealing three large eggs the size of a small boulder. The first one was crimson red, and it had veins growing all around the outer shell. The second one was yellow. And the final one was matte black.

Lady Liv remembered what Kaito had taught her. "Always choose black. Darkness is the absence of light. So in a world without darkness, it would be eternally bright." that's what Kaito had told her. She pointed at the matte black egg.

"We will bring you back to Kaito, lay this egg on the throne. You know what will happen next," the wise man said.

Algar and Aislinn made it to Dragons Rest and were instantly spotted by guards. Instead of running, they stood their ground. There were only four guards. Algar threw his spear into the chest of one of the men, leaving three left.

"Throw me your dagger," Algar shouted to Aislinn. So she threw him the dagger and threw it into another person's face. Killing two of the four guards. The other two rush for Algar, seeing as he has no weapons and is an easy target.

But little do they know Aislinn and Algar have been practicing for this moment. Algar moved Aislinn out of the way, using himself as a shield before Aislinn slid between his legs and ripped straight through the two men's chests.

As soon as the battle ended, Lady Liv and Cassius's followers brought her to the docks.

"What are you two doing here?" Lady Liv asked. Shocked to see her two allies so far away from the frontlines.

"My Lady, we came to save you!" Algar said, shocked to see Lady Liv alive and well.

"I assure you, Lady Liv is in great hands. We are going back to the frontlines, and we are going to fight alongside you and your troops," said the follower of Cassius. Bowing his head to Algar and Aislinn.

"We have to stop this war before it goes any further. Our allies sunk the remainder of Dragons Rest's army. Eldandoor is ours. All there is left is the Forgotten Cities army," Algar said as he helped Lady Liv onboard the ship.

As the ship sailed, the sound of whooshing was heard through the air; the wind picked up and began to get faster and more robust. The water fell an inch or two, and suddenly, a roar was heard.

"It's real… It's really real!" shouted Algar with glee.

A large-grown dragon flew right above the warship.

"It's flying towards the south!" Aislinn said.

The Kaito Harayuma Empire

The roars began to hum overhead. The roars were so violent that they shook the ground beneath them. The ship sailed right behind the dragon, revealing the long tail with what almost seemed like a club at the end of it. Within minutes, the dragon was above the kingdom, roaring and shaking the ground, almost shattering the eardrums of the people below.

Screams erupted from the battlefield. The dragon breathed neon blue flames all over, turning the battlefield and coast into a wildfire, consuming every single man. Enemy forces screamed as they burned alive; the fire was so intense that faces melted due to the heat. Even Kaito's men suffered. Some attempted to dive into the ocean, but the flames were relentless, causing the water to boil instantly.

Oswald and Kaito looked up towards the sky to see the massive blue beast fly overhead and disappear into the sea once again.

"What the hell was that?!" Oswald shouted with excitement.

"That, my friend, was our victory! The Dragon of the Sea," Kaito said.

Everyone who survived shouted with joy and dropped their swords. The month-long battle had finally been won. Nightfall arrived. All the lords, ladies, kings, and queens sat at the long table of The Kaito Harayuma Empire.

"Cheers to a hard-fought victory!" shouted Holden as he clinked his cup against another man's.

"Everyone, we may have won the war, we may have fought a long and hard battle, but we owe it all to that dragon. We must relocate before Dragons Rest and The Forgotten City can rebuild their forces and launch a stronger attack. It's our time to dominate the South!" Kaito exclaimed before tossing back his ale.

Lady Liv stood in the throne room, placing her egg on the throne. Cassius appeared behind her.

"We won the battle, but the Desolation is still upon us," Cassius said, his dark, cold gaze fixed on Lady Liv.

"You are to have a child with Kaito; it will be a boy, and you will name him Bjorne," Cassius continued, still looking at Lady Liv's stomach. "You chose the right man, and he will lead you to glory."
"Who are you?" Lady Liv asked, perplexed by the sudden appearance of this man in her castle.

"I am Cassius, the right hand of Thornos," he replied.

Lady Liv understood the gravity of the situation and agreed to Cassius's plan.

"Your husband… your king… is the King of Desolation," Cassius stated before walking out of the room, disappearing in a pillar of ash.

Later, Kaito entered the room.

"My Lady, we have emerged victorious over our enemies. You now rule your kingdom. Shall we celebrate a little?"

Sun Crest

Lord Getano and his men sailed home, knowing Prince Bjarne would be close behind him. Cassius appeared on the island of Sun Crest.

"You will die today, alongside your family, protecting your home. A single man will end your tribe, and no one can stop it," Cassius said, his stare carrying the weight of impending death, aimed directly at Lord Getano.

"How could this be possible? We are just noblemen, and have nothing to do with any past or present war," Lord Getano said, fearing for his life.

Cassius walked away, fading into ash once more. An hour passed, and life on Sun Crest resumed as normal. Lord Getano thought Cassius had been lying. He didn't know who he was.

A single rowboat appeared at Sun Crest's small dock. Lord Getano went to see who it was, expecting a nobleman returning from a fishing trip. To his surprise, it was Prince Bjarne. They locked eyes briefly before Prince Bjarne drew his sword and charged at Lord Getano. Lord Getano tried to draw his weapon, but it was too late; the sword had already pierced his stomach. Lord Getano fell to his knees.

"Why? Why do this to me and my people?" Lord Getano asked, hoping to stir sympathy in the prince.

"You betrayed me, killed a hundred of my men, and now I will kill all three hundred of your men, all your children, and all your women," Prince Bjarne said, pulling the sword from Lord Getano's stomach, preparing to swing for his neck.

"Goodbye, traitor," Prince Bjarne said before beheading Lord Getano. Prince Bjarne ventured further into the island, familiar with its layout from previous visits. The children knew and respected him, some even considering him family.

A child approached Prince Bjarne and hugged his leg. Prince Bjarne looked down at the child and grinned as he grabbed a dagger from his waist and plunged it into the child's head. The child did not die immediately; the dagger remained in his head. The child looked up at Prince Bjarne.

"What did we do to deserve this?" the child asked.

"Your father is a traitor, and now you all must suffer," Prince Bjarne grinned as he pulled the dagger from the boy's head, blood spraying on his face. He wiped it off, revealing a sinister grin. His rampage was not over yet, and it would not end until every household on Sun Crest was extinguished.

He continued towards the village and reached a small forest where an old man lived, a close friend of King Raeder who helped build homes in Dragons Rest. Prince Bjarne approached the door and knocked politely. The old man opened the door.

"Prince Bjarne, what are you doing here at this hour?" the old nobleman asked.

The prince did not reply but looked at the man and smiled before plunging his sword through the old, rotting wood door and into the man's liver. The man fell. Prince Bjarne entered the home and climbed on top of the old man. He had gone completely mad. He plunged the bloodied dagger he used to kill the child into the man's throat and pulled it out, leaving the old man to bleed out on his floor.

Prince Bjarne took a torch from the man's wall, igniting a part of the rotting door. The fire spread quickly through the dry, old wood, engulfing the forest around it. Nightfall descended, and it was the perfect time for the prince to go door to door in the village.

He kicked down the door of the first house and found two babies, not more than a few months old. He grabbed one from the bassinet. It was sound asleep, unaware of the impending horror. He smashed the baby's head against the sharp corner connecting two rooms, repeating until the baby's face was unrecognizable.

The first baby's screams woke the second. Prince Bjarne seized the knife from the father's bedside table and plunged it into the second baby's tiny heart, killing it swiftly. The parents woke, but the father was defenseless; the prince had his knife. The prince threw the knife into the father's stomach. As the man and woman cried, Prince Bjarne knocked over an oil lamp from the bedside table.

"Do not cry. It will be over quickly," he said as the house erupted in flames. He

walked outside, watching the man and woman burn with joy. He proceeded to the next house, where a family of four stood outside in shock.
Prince Bjarne walked over to the family.

"I tried to save them, but I was too late," he said, feigning sorrow as the woman hugged him. The prince grabbed his dagger and stabbed the woman in the side. As he withdrew the sword, she collapsed.

The father picked up his three-year-old son and ran as the other kid ran behind them. Prince Bjarne's bloody hunt quickened. He tackled the boy, who was too far from his father. "Your daddy left you behind, boy. It is time you die," he said, thrusting his dagger into the boy's leg and standing over him. "If you can make it to your daddy, I'll let you live," he said, but the child still tried to crawl away, screaming out to his father. "He can't save you. He's weak, just like you," said the prince.

Prince Bjarne has a maniacal smile on his face as he stands on the boy's back and bends over to his face. The dagger ran deep into the boy's back. He pulls it out and wipes the blood from it before doing it again. And again... And again.

"You see this daddy? This is what happens when you obey the orders of a traitor," Prince Bjarne says as he holds the young boy by the hair. "I will butcher every single one of you. I will put you down like pigs."

The father doesn't even try to run. He runs towards the prince, screaming out in anger. But before he gets close enough to reach the prince... The prince takes a step forward and stabs the man in the lung with his sword.

"I'll let you suffer," he says, grinning as he walks away. The child he set down began to bawl his eyes out. "I hate whiners," he said to the child before beheading it.

The prince walks back towards the town and grabs another torch lit with the fire from the already burning home. He sees a guard holding a bow aimed at his face.

"You can try and shoot that thing, but you're not going to hit your target!" The prince shouted. The cold, dead gaze of the prince brought fear and anguish into the guard's body.

"Kill yourself, do me a solid, and stab yourself in the heart. I guarantee it will be less painful if you do it than if I do it to you." Prince Bjarne didn't think he would do it. But the man grabbed a knife from his waist and dug it into his heart. The man fell to his knees and bled out.

Prince Bjarne had two more important houses on his list before he left, the first one being an inventor who fled Dragons Rest after killing Prince Bjarne's mother. The second is a young assassin that the prince helped escape his duties of assassinating his best friend.

Prince Bjarne walked up to the first home, kicked down the door, and walked inside. He saw the man who killed his mother lying there fast asleep.

"Wake up! Get up! Now!" Prince Bjarne screamed as he shook the man awake.

"What is it?" asked the inventor. It took him a moment to realize who shook him awake, but when he did, he grabbed a knife and backed himself into the corner of the room.

"What do you want from me?!" the inventor asked.

"You killed my mother! She was pregnant! You kill my sibling inside the womb! And for that, I will take your life." The prince was not trying to be quiet anymore. He did not care who heard him.

As Prince Bjarne walked closer and closer to the man, the man started flailing his knife around, cutting into the prince's arm. But that didn't stop the prince. He continued to walk towards the man. Prince Bjarne hit his glove against the knife, throwing it to the ground. The man ducked down to grab it, but it was already too late.

Prince Bjarne began to stab the man, carving him open like a beast. The man was left in the corner of his room, gutted. His organs were strung out of his body. Prince Bjarne laughed, clearing the blood from his dagger as he walked out of the room and toward his next target.

The Prince walked towards the edge of the island, where a beautiful vacation home sat. Prince Bjarne walked up the stairs to the door and knocked. It swung open. When the prince walked to the man's room, he was already dead. He stabbed himself in the heart, and it looked as if he was dead for days. A note sat next to him.

"The world is over as we know it. Thornos cannot save us. It is to Prince Bjarne I owe my life and death."

Prince Bjarne walked out of the house, burning each house as he went along. By the time he was done, He walked out of the village with large plumes of smoke rising behind him. He washed his face in the water from the sea. And got into his boat.

"Your next Father."

The Kaito Harayuma Empire

Kaito Harayuma, Cenric Hayes, Holden Hayes, Kenelm Randem, Algar Forde, Oswald Edgare, Lady Olivia Of Eldandoor, Queen Saga of Mystria, Aislinn Wildarde, Seraphina FireSong, Emberlyn Firesong, and Avalon FireSong are all seated in the grand planning hall.

"We have won the war, but now it is time for the hardest one of all. The rebuilding of the south," Kaito says.

"FireSong family, your ride to the ruins of Ember Fall. Rebuild as much as you can, and recruit surrounding villages to help. Devil's bandits and Lady Liv, you are with me. We are marching to the dead city. We are going to take the city of the dead for ourselves. Queen Saga, you must return to your people and rebuild from the attack of Eldandoor," Kaito says, pointing at key points on the table and moving pawns around.

"We have word that Sun Crest has fallen; it is in shambles, and there are no survivors," Oswald says, putting his head down towards the table.

"That's a shame, and they were a great ally in our war. Any idea who did it?" Lady Liv asked.

"He has the nickname the human butcher. It is unknown who did it, but they are highly dangerous," Oswald said, horrified by the thought of an infant killer on the loose.

"Do you think you can take The City of the Dead, just the seven of you?" asked Queen Saga.

"The dead are already dead. It should be quite simple," Kaito said, showing no fear in the battle against the dead.

Everyone in the room splits off into their assigned groups.

Dragons Rest

Prince Bjarne arrived at Dragons Rest by sunrise. He walked towards the gates. The guards stood there, not moving a muscle.

"You are not welcome here, Bjarne," said one of the guards.

"I am Prince Bjarne from the kingdom of Dragons Rest, Son of King Raeder," the prince shouted out.

"Take another step towards these gates, and you will be shot down," the guard shouted out before drawing his bow. All the other guards drew theirs as well.

Prince Bjarne knew he had to find another way in, so he walked away and got into his boat. He sailed a few miles around the shore of the mountainous kingdom and found the one weakness nobody had ever noticed. A large mountain led right behind the castle, and a rockslide had left an entrance through the wall.

Prince Bjarne knew how weak the kingdom was due to the war in the south. As he climbed where the rockslide was, he knew this could be his last day on earth or his first day as the ruler of Dragons Rest. He climbed over the wall and saw two boys playing. They looked at Prince Raeder, excited to see him back home.

The two boys ran up to Raeder. "Where have you been?" they asked.

"I have killed an entire empire. And this one is next. How about you two help me?" he said, grinning from ear to ear.

"Tell us what to do, and we will do it!" the boys were eager to help their favorite person in all of Nastomar.

"See the guards in front of the castle, run up to them and stab them with these knives," he said as he handed over two knives.

The two boys and the prince walked close to the guards, and the two kids ran at them quickly, stabbing them repeatedly. The guards screamed out as the alarm bells rang. A group of guards comes running towards the two kids, and the two kids are brutally shot and stabbed by the guards, leaving them to bleed out all over the stairs in front of the castle, dying for their prince. But it left enough time for Prince Bjarne to walk past the guards and into the castle.

When he entered, three guards waited for him. They all rushed towards the prince, but before the prince could even draw his sword, one of the guards swung for his head. It sliced the surface of his face just enough to draw blood. But it wasn't enough to stop the prince. The prince quickly pulled out a dagger and stabbed the noble guard in the stomach. He twisted the knife 360 degrees before pulling it out. "That leaves two of you," he said, grinning.

The first one tried to take a head-on approach, continuously swinging his sword back and forth, side to side. Prince Bjarne could tell this guard was inexperienced and would probably fail to stand if Prince Bjarne dodged his attack. So that is what he did. Perfectly timed a block from the guard's frantic swings, knocking the guard back. Prince Bjarne lunged forward, stabbing the guard through the heart with his sword. But without any time to recover from that parry, the other guard ran behind him. Quickly, the prince noticed this and moved out of the way, leaving that guard to tumble down the stairs, breaking his neck on the way down.

"By the gods, why did we hire such idiots," the prince mumbled to himself as he dusted himself off. He had six more floors to clear of guards before he made it to his father's chambers.

Prince Bjarne walked into the first-floor Grand Hall, where some of the Lords and Ladies of Nastomar were feasting while talking about Sun Crest's mysterious murders.

"Ah, Prince Bjarne. We would like your opinion on this matter," says Lord Chadwicke of Winter Crest.

"Well, Lord Chadwicke, I believe the man responsible for the murders has a more serious agenda. I believe Dragons Rest is next," the prince struck confusion into the six Lords and seven ladies who sat around this large table.

Lord Chadwicke knew what he meant. He slid his chair back and quickly ran towards the Prince. "Goodbye, Lord Chadwicke," he said before throwing a knife into his right eye with insane precision.

The rest of the Lords and ladies stood up and drew their weapons. They were ready to fight to the death. And they would be fighting to the death. They all stood in different places in the room, waiting for the prince to make a move.

Prince Bjarne walked over to the lit fire in the chimney. He grabbed a pouch from his waist and threw it into the fire. The fire roared, and the Lords and ladies screamed out, knowing what was about to happen. The furnace erupted into flames, and a large explosion happened right after Prince Bjarne escaped. He heard the screams of the Lords and ladies behind him as the roof began to cave in.

"Pathetic, really. Nobody can even hurt me," Prince Bjarne was disappointed at the fact that nobody had stopped his efforts even though he was hardly trying at all.

He walks slowly up the stairs to the second of six floors. A bigger group of guards stood at the top of the stairs. Three of them had bows, and two of them had sickles. The three bowmen fired at the prince, but all three missed. Prince Bjarne was behind them before they could realize it.
Prince Bjarne had a dagger in each hand and stabbed two of the three archers in the back of the heads, using his knees to push their

bodies off the daggers and down the stairs. One of the archers got lucky, firing an arrow into Prince Bjarne's collarbone.

"Your aim is amazing. If you survive this, I might even knight you," he said jokingly before ripping the arrow out of his collarbone and shoving it into the bowmen's mouth. Forcing the man's jaws open and shoving the arrow straight through the back of his mouth.

The two men with sickles charged towards the prince. But one of them missed and fell directly through the second-story window, falling into a fiery kingdom below. The other man, however, got lucky and was able to hit the prince in the same place he was recently stabbed, re-opening the wound.

The prince winced in pain before he grabbed the man's face and shoved his thumbs into the man's eye sockets, bursting the eyeballs. Leaving him blinded and bleeding before he began beating the man repetitively.

Meanwhile, Randel was running through the chaotic streets of Dragon Rest as the sound of the alarm bells rang, and ash and debris rained down on the kingdom lower than the mountainous castle. The houses and merchant stall caught fire right before Randels's eyes. He knew he must protect his father and repay the debt that he owed him.

Randel ran towards the castle, running from fires and explosions left and right. Citizens were begging for help. Some pleaded to the gods, begging them not to let them die in such a pathetic way.

Randel got to the bottom of the first-floor stairs and heard the crackling of the fire from the floor above him. He ran through the fire up the second flight of stairs. There, he was met by Prince Bjarne.

"You know, brother, I can't let you walk out of here alive. You are the rightful heir to the Dragon Rest throne," the Prince said, holding his sword in one hand and pointing towards Randel.

"I never wanted it. You know that," a nobleman working in the third-floor library attempted to run past the prince, but swiftly, the prince stuck out his right arm and stuck the librarian with the pointy end of his dagger. Pulling it out immediately, leaving the man to die in a pool of his blood at the prince's feet.

"Why?! Why kill so many people? Why kill me and father?!" Randel shouted out at Prince Bjarne.

"Because you two don't see the world the way I see it. Everyone who has died by my hands was scum. If they were stronger, they would have survived," Prince Bjarne says, still pointing his sword towards Randel, who is slowly moving his way to an opening of the staircase.

"I am unarmed, Bjarne. Spare me, and I will help you clean up this mess," Randel said, begging his brother to spare him.

"How pathetic, asking your brother to spare your life. Get on the ground," Prince Bjarne said.

Randel got on his knees with tears running down his face. "You are a traitor to our family," Randel said before the long sword was ripping straight through his face.

Prince Bjarne ripped the sword out of his brother's face, feeling no remorse for the actions he had done. On the third floor, the prince was met with seven of Dragons Rest's best fighters.

"C'mon, let's get this over with," Prince Bjarne said as he ran into the group of men. Two of the men were instantly defeated by the blade that the prince carried.

The strength behind Prince Bjarne's swings has increased several times since the first battle he faced, and he had to try this time. Somehow, one single man was able to corner five men.

The castle was beginning to crumble, and there was a massive gaping hole in the wall. "Goodbye warriors," Prince Randel said as he grinned and pushed on the man in the front, consequently causing him to tumble into all the other men, knocking them to their deaths.

The rest of the floors were a breeze, barely guarded at all. But when the prince reached the roof of the castle, his father stood at the edge, watching the chaos unfold beneath him.

"I have been waiting for you, son," The king said, not even turning to look at his son.

"Does it feel liberating to kill thousands of innocent people?" asked the king.

"It does. And you are the last person I will kill before I take over Nastomar," Prince Bjarne said, closing in behind King Raeder.

"Father, please put up a good fight," Prince Bjarne said as he threw his sword to the side.

King Raeder turned around and threw his sword off the side of the castle as well. "Only one of us will make it out alive. I know I have lost, but that won't stop me from trying," they both stood about three feet away from each other, staring into each other's souls.

King Raeder lunged forward, throwing his fist toward Prince Raeder with insane speed. It didn't matter, of course. His son was better than him in hand-to-hand combat. Swing after swing, Prince Bjarne dodged. And he finally decided to fight back, swinging and hitting his father in the head, knocking the crown to the side.

"One day, that crown will be mine," Prince Bjarne said as he threw another punch into his father's stomach, knocking King Raeder to his knees.

"It is already your son," King Raeder said as he stood up, hitting an uppercut onto Prince Bjarne's chin.

As Prince Bjarne stood up, he spit the blood out of his mouth. Prince Bjarne lunged forward, swinging his fists closer and closer to King Raeder. But eventually, he ran out of breath, leaving the opportunity for King Raeder to strike.

King Raeder tackled Prince Bjarne to the ground and began beating his son. But before he knew it, he was bleeding out beside his son. Prince Bjarne remembered what his father taught him as a young prince.

"If you can't win fair, play dirty." Prince Bjarne was hiding a dagger in his waist belt. Before he fell to the ground, he stuck it up, and when King Raeder fell out of breath and laid on top of his son, the blade went straight through him.

Prince Bjarne stood up and drug his father's bleeding corpse to the end of the castle roof. "That was a fun yet pitiful attempt, Father. May Thornos bring you peace and happiness," Prince Bjarne said as he kicked his father's body off of the edge of the castle. Sending it flying down into the middle of the burning kingdom.

Seraphina

Seraphina FireSong went a separate way from her two younger siblings. Seraphina went further south of the ruins of Ember Fall to a town known as Persepolis, run by Lord Cyrus, who has quite a great sum of gold and jewelry. Seraphina came to Persepolis to gain some more coins to hire builders and men to repair Ember Fall. As she rode into the town, the gates opened, and right in the front of the kingdom sat Lord Cyrus, attending to his geese.

Lord Cyrus was a tall, chubby man with a long ginger beard. "Seraphina! Long time no see! How have you been?"

"I have been good, Uncle Cyrus!" Seraphina exclaimed, giving her uncle a warm, welcoming hug.

"Come with me, I'm sure you are tired from your journey here. Come see your cousins and Aunt Jemma!" Lord Cyrus said.

Lord Cyrus is such a warm and inviting man until you bring him into battle; when he is in battle, fighting for a noble cause, he is a beast, a killing machine. But

Seraphina wouldn't have to worry about that. The war was already over.

Seraphina walked into the living room of Lord Cyrus's home. On one wall was the head of a dire wolf that was passed down through all the generations of the family. And on the other wall was the sigil of the Nastomar bank. Lord Cyrus's great-great-great-grandfather had started the Nastomar Bank when he was still alive. And the family Cyrus has kept it running ever since.

A small, thinner lady with long red hair walked into the room with a little boy hiding between her legs. "Seraphina!! It is such an honor to see you again!" Aunt Jemma said. Aunt Jemma and Uncle Cyrus met twenty years ago on the battlefield in the war against the dead city. They were two of the only survivors to live long, prosperous lives after the battle.

"This is Percy, our firstborn son." Uncle Cyrus said. Percy was a young boy just now learning to walk.

"Now, what was it you came to Persepolis?" asked Lord Cyrus, setting down a cup of warm snowberry tea in front of Seraphina.

"We need help. Our king has asked us to rebuild Ember Fall, but we cannot do such a thing without people and money," Seraphina calmly explained.

"And why doesn't he come to meet us on this wonderful fall day?" asked Uncle Cyrus.

"He and some of his most entrusted men are taking back the City of the Dead," Seraphina said nervously, chuckling to herself.

"There is no possible way you think only a small group of men can take back that city, and it has been gone for centuries," Aunt Jemma said, laughing at Seraphina, thinking she is playing a joke.

"'Tis not funny, Aunty; he is followed by the Devil's Bandits. I am sure they will take back the city somehow or another," Seraphina stood tall with the words she spoke because she truly believed in her king.

"I can send men your way and lend some coin, but you better be backing the right horse. We know how dangerous the world is right now," Uncle Cyrus was a fair man, and he gave Seraphina a group of thirty men and a few hundred gold coins to pay some workers.

"Before you leave, we have some questions for you. And we need you to be honest with us," Aunt Jemma said after she put Percy back in his room to play with a wooden elk.

"Is it true, this king of yours is of Harayuma descent?" asked Aunt Jemma.

"He is the final Harayuma remaining," Seraphina said, confused.

"You are aware his family is the reason you have no home anymore?" Uncle Cyrus said, questioning Seraphina's choices.

"We will have a home after we rebuild it," Seraphina said, trying to stay calm.

"You said he is working with the Devil's bandits. Is he also going to marry Lady Liv of Eldandoor?" Aunt Jemma asked.

"The wedding will be in Ember Fall after it is rebuilt. We don't plan on inviting many people, but if I heard the rumor correctly, there would be a monster present," Seraphina said, hinting at the return of the now King Bjarne of Dragons Keep.

"Do you know anything about the human butcher?" asked Seraphina, still curious about who the mystery person was.

"We have insider information telling us that the human butcher is indeed Prince Bjarne, who is now king of Dragons Keep. He butchered not only all of the people of Sun Crest but ninety percent of the people in Dragons Keep. I fear we will be his next targets, seeing as most of the south's army are either dead or weakened," Uncle Cyrus said, twiddling his fingers anxiously.

"We won't let him conquer the south, Kaito Harayuma won't let him come near us. If he does, he will fall quickly and painfully," Seraphina says, getting up from her seat and walking back to her horse.

"Thank you for your help, uncle," she says before riding back to Ember Fall.

Aislinn

Aislinn stayed in The Kaito Harayuma Empire, watching as Kaito and his party left for The Dead City. Aislinn was left with one job: watch over the egg and keep the people of the empire safe.

Aislinn stood in the throne room, waiting for the egg to do something. "Man, this egg is boring. It just looks like a rock," Aislinn mumbled under her breath.

A young man walked through the door and sat at the edge of the steps leading to the throne. "So you are the war commander?" asked the young boy.

"That is correct…. Hey, I've seen you before. Did you fight in the war?" she asked.

"I did. That's how I lost this," he said as he pulled up his sleeve, revealing a stub where his left hand would be.

"I'm sorry. I didn't know," Aislinn said.

"You know, the main reason I fought in that war was because of you. You are so strong and beautiful. I know you have important duties now, but I thought we could talk and share some stories while we wait for that rock to do something. My name is Aleron, but you can just call me Al."

Aleron was Aislinn's age. Although he was much taller than Aislinn, he was missing his left hand, and he had a massive scar across his right eye.

"Well, Al, my name is Aislinn, and you are quite handsome for a one-handed man," Aislinn said, joking around with her new friend.

"You know, Aislinn, I heard you killed Tully Dueani. How did that feel?" asked Aleron, eager to hear what Aislinn had to say.

"Well, it was my first kill that seemed real. The rest of the kills were easy. Most of the men were dumb and caught off guard. But Tully, she never wanted to hurt me. I don't feel bad killing her, no… I did it for my king and my country," Aislinn said, her voice emanating from the past.

"I didn't have much experience fighting in the war, but we fought side by side once; that's how I got this sword. He had a huge saber. He had to have been from the forgotten city. Tall blonde-haired man. Sliced my face clean open," Aleron rubbed his fingers over the deep scar across his face.

"I remember that. I slit his throat. The blood of that man puddled at our feet," Aislinn said.

"So your job is seriously to wait and watch this rock?" asked Aleron.

"Yes. It is supposedly a dragon's egg," Aislinn said, staring at the sleek matte black egg.

Aleron stood up and touched the egg. "It feels like wet leather. Kind of gross if you ask me," Aleron said.

"Hey, I have a question for you, Al… do you want to go to the wedding with me in Ember Fall?"

"I would love to, as long as I'm invited," Aleron said, smiling at Aislinn, looking into her beautiful blue eyes.

Aislinn could see him looking at her. "Do you like what you see?" she said, giggling.

"Why yes—of course, I do," Aleron said, his stomach filled with butterflies. He leaned in to kiss Aislinn, but right as their lips touched behind them, the sounds of a cracking eggshell were heard.

Aislinn and Aleron stood up quickly and watched as a baby dragon emerged from the slimy insides of the matte black egg. The dragon crawled out of the egg, and Aislinn noticed a letter sitting on the arm of the throne. It read, "Dear Aislinn if by chance this egg happens to hatch, I want you to keep it. We need more powerful warriors like you, much luv. Lady Olivia."

"Liv wants me to keep it," Aislinn said to Aleron, who was already trying to touch the dragon. The dragon matched the egg. It was matte black with sleek scales and crimson-red eyes.

Aleron finally gathered the courage to touch the dragon, but as he touched it, it zapped him with electricity. Although it wasn't visible to the naked eye, the dragon emitted a strong electric current. Aislinn picked it up and looked underneath it.

"It's a girl. I will name her Inessa," the dragon roared, though it sounded more like a groan. Inessa means pure of heart or clean. Aislinn chose this name because she wanted the world to be pure and clean for her king, and she and her dragon would cleanse the world of hatred and evil no matter what it took.

Aislinn leaned in to kiss Aleron for the second time, and the dragon flew onto her shoulder. She may be young still, but she is now the mother of a beautiful dragon.

"Inessa will grow to be quite large if the books I have read are true," Aleron said.

"Yes, I know. It's unbelievable that a boy like me reads books, but honestly, I quite enjoy reading. It's peaceful," Aleron said, smiling as he held his face close to Aislinn's.

"That's cute. You're the brains, and I'm the brawn. It just works," Aislinn said, nuzzling her nose against Aleron's.

"How about we take this baby outside? I'm sure it would like to see the sun," Aislinn said as she and Aleron held hands and walked outside of the throne room.

It was a nice day out. The weather was changing. However, winter was nearing, getting closer and closer by the day.

"Winter will be here soon," Aleron said.

"Winter is my least favorite season, and it brings famine and death," Aislinn said.

"You remind me a lot of winter, Aislinn, beautiful, and not to mention the death part," Aleron said, laughing at his joke.

"See, I'm funny too," Aleron said, leaning in for another kiss.

Dragons Rest

The now King Bjarne rules over what is left of Dragons Rest. The kingdom that once had nearly a million citizens now only has twenty-six thousand inhabitants. King Dueani sails overseas to the destroyed city. The city is burnt to the ground, covered in ash. King Bjarne doesn't have much to rule over, seeing as the kingdom is in ruins.

King Bjarne meets King Dueani at the gates of the kingdom. "Your grace. Thanks for coming," Bjarne says as he bends the knee to the opposing king.

"This place looks like hell. Was this your work?" asked King Dueani, in total awe of the amount of destruction caused to his allied city.

"This was indeed my doing, for good reason, too," said King Bjarne.

"And that reason being?" asked King Dueani.

"The people of this city were traitors, following a king who wanted power. I do not seek out power, and I seek out prosperity and cleanliness," King Bjarne said as he took a step forward away from the docks.

"Come now, you have much to see," King Bjarne urged.

As they walked, burnt corpses littered the streets, and the splashing and squishing of guts and corpses felt wet and slimy on the boots of the two kings.

"The people of this city were weak. I'll give it a few months, and the city will be returned to its former glory," King Bjarne said.

"You butchered nearly a million innocent people. You have truly gone mad," King Dueani said.

"Yes, well, this is not what you came here for. I need your help with one final thing. We must eliminate one last kingdom, send your men to the gates of Frost Fall, and we shall reign victorious over half of the world," King Bjarne said, still walking through the streets.

The men inched closer and closer to King Raeder's corpse. As they make it, the charred corpse sits there, its face burnt and unrecognizable, the armor burnt into his body, leaving a metallic shine to the rest of his corpse. And one large chunk of flesh was missing from his arm.

"I will send my men, your grace," King Dueani says.

"Wait before you leave; take this gift. The finest meat in all of Nastomar. Eat this when you return home. I assure you, you won't regret it," he handed over a tiny box filled to the brim with what looked like charred pig skin.

King Dueani nodded, walked back to his ship, and sailed away.

Cassius

Cassius stood in the rubble of Ember Fall. Standing underneath the fallen chapel, the roof had caved in, but it still held up enough to protect the insides from destruction.

"He is coming to Frost Fall," Cassius said, talking to a curtain in the ruined chapel. The curtain was straight black but had two purple dots in the center of it. The curtain was twelve feet tall and used to hold a statue of Thornos.

"Give me guidance, Thornos," Cassius said. "Sun Crest will rise again. They will fend the enemy forces away from Frost's fall long enough for the enemies to fall. When it is done, the ghosts will be laid to rest."

A long grumble shook the chapel. Dust rolled down from the ceiling.

"Thank you, Thornos," Cassius said as he bowed and turned away.

After Cassius walked far enough away, a twelve-foot-tall, sleek black creature with dark purple eyes emerged. Its teeth were stained with blood. It almost looked human. It laughed to itself.

"I can't keep hiding. This Kaito human makes it hard to stay quiet." His words were quiet; nobody else could hear them, yet they were so loud. Loud enough to shake the ground beneath him.

Meanwhile, on the other side of Ember Fall, The FireSong Family met once again. They sat on top of their horses quite some ways from the ruins. They all stood tall and strong. Behind each of the three stood a large number of men, each ready to get to work on the kingdom at hand. A small plume of dark smoke was seen behind them for a moment before fading away again.

Seraphina, Emberyln, and Avalon all sat on top of their horses. "So this is what we were able to pay for?" asked Seraphina, pointing towards the group of builders.

"Yeah, about six hundred of them," Emberyln said, not very happy with the small amount of people they were able to pay.

"The people I have spoken with say this could be finished enough in nine months. Or at least finished enough to move some people back in," Avalon said happily. Avalon was keen on slow thoughts when it came to war and seasons.

"This means we will have to work all through the winter season. We don't know how long winter can be, and the last winter almost took a full year to end," Seraphina said, fiddling with her fingers on top of her horse.

"And another issue, the human butcher is still out there. If he comes south… well, the south is defenseless at this very moment," Emberyln said, worried about the South's integrity.

"We must not worry about the future, and we are in the hands of the gods. What we must worry about is Lady Liv and Kaito. They are about to face one of the worst battles they will ever face," Avalon said, having some knowledge about the Dead City.

"I'm sure they will be fine, but what worries me is the news that Lady Liv is pregnant with Kaito's child," Emberyln said worryingly.

"And yet he still allowed her to fight in this battle—" Seraphina started to say before being cut off by Avalon.

"Hey, did you two see those thin plumes of smoke coming from Ember Fall?" Avalon said, looking up in the sky at a massive plume of what seemed to be black ash floating in the sky.

The Dead City

Lady Olivia, King Kaito Harayuma, and all the members of the Devil's bandits make it to the dead city at dusk. It was one of the most dangerous times to be around the dead city. The closer they got to the dead city, the moans and screams grew.

"My Lords, my Lady, a lot lies in our hands for this battle. If we all make it out alive, I will knight every one of you." Kaito had a serious look on his face. "I won't lie to you. You guys are the closest thing I have to family, and I cannot afford to lose family." Kaito looked at Lady Liv and put his hand on her stomach, looking at her with a serious look on his face. As they rode in through the outskirts of the town. This city was said to have been cursed by a witch hundreds of years ago. A witch was angered by the king and placed a curse over the city so that everyone living there was split into three groups of undead, lurkers. The main group isn't slow or necessarily strong unless they are in a large group. Rushers, the ones that will bolt for the humans and devour them within seconds. And the tanks, giant beasts that could crush a man into a pile of dust within a second.

A large feral cat walked by. It stopped in the middle of the road and mewed. Within a second, at least twenty dead men leaped out of the shadows and began feasting on the cat.

"There are only two ways to get the jump on these monsters. Aim for the head and aim for the arms. If he cuts the head off their bodies, they won't be able to use their body. And if we cut their arms off, all they will have is their heads." Oswald said as they all stared into the pile of undead.

None of the members had torches, but it was a stormy night. A lighting flash lit up the city and the party. The undead must have seen them through the lighting flashes. The group of undead stood up, twisting their necks backward. Between the lightning flashes, the group could tell that this would be a long battle.

The group of twenty undead men ran full speed towards the group of humans. Kaito drew his sword and charged in with his horse, only to be immediately swarmed by the undead. They didn't even try to hurt Kaito; instead, they began to rip into the flesh of the horse, eating through its stomach. The horse screamed in pain as Kaito ripped the undead off the horse, stabbing and slicing through them over and over.

A sudden howl was heard from further into town. Dark red eyes began to emerge. It was the most dangerous type of undead, one only seen twice before. A howler. When a howler screams, it attracts all nearby dead men to attack. Hundreds of undead ran through the city streets towards Kaito.

Oswald and his men charged in attempting to stop them from reaching Kaito. Algar was the first off of his horse, smacking it on the rump, spooking it, and sending it running off away from the scene of the battle. Algar drew his spear and began spinning it, blocking fists away from his body.

Next off his horse was Cenric. He grabbed the warhammer off of his horse and began crushing heads. Kaito was able to get to his feet and get his sword back again. One undead rushed for Lady Liv, who was in shock, sitting still on top of her horse. The undead man was fast. It leaped onto Lady

Liv, and it began to tear into the armor protecting her stomach.

Kaito screamed in anger and threw his dark steel sword right into the rotted head of the monster. Sending it to the ground lifeless once more.

"You must leave. It is not safe for you here." Kaito said, helping Lady Liv back onto her horse.

"I want to fight my king, and I want to help!" Lady Liv shouted as Kaito hit the horse, sending it running back toward the Kaito Harayuma empire.

The undead began to swarm the Devil's bandits.

"We must move to the rooftops!" shouted Kaito as he darted towards the roof of an abandoned brothel. Every member of the devil's bandits followed suit.

"How well do the dead deal with fire?" Kaito asked, lighting an arrow with a torch.

"Let us find out!" Oswald shouted as he also loaded his bow with a firing arrow.

They all shot down on the undead with fire arrow after fire arrow, lighting them all on fire. They sat on that roof until morning came up.

The undead are weaker during the sun's time because the sun weakens their eyes. It's more easy for humans to hide away from the undead during the day. As the first rays of daybreak shone over the dead city. The undead began to falter. Their movements began to slow, and some even collapsed onto one another as the sunlight burned into their rotting flesh.

The party was battered but still in good condition. The undead had devoured all their horses.

"We have no means of escape." Oswald said, looking below at the crowd of undead people.

"Guess we'll have to fight then." Kaito said, setting down the bow beside him.

Kaito looked at his fellow warriors with a sense of relief. " We have made it through the night, but this fight is far from over. The deeper we get into this city, the more the undead army will meet us." Kaito said, watching over the looks of his fellow man.

The party cautiously descended from the top of the roof, slaying the group of undead easily now that they were slowed.

Lady Olivia came rushing in on her horse. "You seriously thought I would leave you behind?" she giggled as she hopped off her horse before it even came to a complete stop. She jumped into the hands of Kaito. "My love, I rode to Mystria, and a group of men rode behind me."

Lady Liv was a smart girl with a hundred men, and they could take the city by nightfall. Kaito embraced Lady Liv's warm hug. Relieved to not only see that she was alive but also to see that she brought men without even being asked.

"Good thinking, princess. We need all the help we can get. Let us make our way deeper into the city and meet up with the men." Kaito said he was proud of his soon-to-be wife and queen. A few months ago, she was just a lost princess trapped in the keep by his father and uncle. Now, she has become one of the most powerful women in the realm of Nastomar.

The party met up with the group that rode in on horseback.

"Men, you know what's at stake here? We must make it to the keep in the center of the town and kill the king of the undead.

Once that is done, the curse will be lifted, and all the other undead will be finished off." Kaito said, looking into the heart of the city.

The party of a hundred and thirty men marched into the unknown city. The streets were narrow and carried the stench of decay, strong enough to make the nose hairs burn. The howls and tongue clicks of the undead rung out along the city's alleys and buildings. The sounds were enough to fill the warriors with an off-putting feeling and the feeling of dread.

As they got deeper, the amount of small battles increased. At one point, the men were surrounded. But Kaito, with his swift movements, was able to fend off all of them practically on his own.

It was nightfall once again, and the party made it to the city's keep.

"Men, stay outside. Lady Liv will protect you and lead you." The Devil's Bandits and I will clear the keep of all the undead.

The men walked into the keep, but there, surprisingly, was nothing. Until they made it to the deepest part of the keep. There sat a tall creature. It held the form of a deer, but as it stood up, it showed the arms of a human and the legs of a spider. And the undead skull of an elk.

"Fuck, this thing is ugly." Holden said, not wanting anything to do with the battle to come.

The creature walked closer and closer to the men. Algar drew his spear and pointed it towards the creature, keeping it from coming any closer. Oswald pulled out his war axe, preparing to charge into battle. Holden pointed his long bow at the head of the creature. Cenric drew his war hammer, and Kaito drew his sword.

Holden shot at the head of the creature, hitting it in the eye, but within a second, the creature ripped the arrow out and charged closer to Oswald. Oswald gave Algar a nod and rushed towards the legs of the creature, swinging his axe and chopping off two of the legs. The legs poofed into a cloud of smoke, and the creature tipped over. Cenric rushed in, hitting the creature in the back of the head with his war hammer. But the creature took to blow like it was nothing. The two legs that Oswald chopped off had grown back already, and the creature adjusted itself back to the upright position.

Kaito ran past Algar's spear and sliced into the skinny left arm. Blood splatted all over the room as the bottom half of the arm shriveled up. But it was no ordinary blood; this blood was black and looked like oil.

"This is a losing battle!" shouted Algar, backing away from the monster.

The monster rushed forward, lunging at Kaito. Luckily,Kaito was able to move in time, leaving the creature to smash through the wall into the other room. The party of warriors stood in front of the massive gaping hole to see the creature crawl out of the rubble and stand back up. It screeched loudly, and everyone in the keep's ears began to drip blood. The ears rang so loudly that there was no way of communicating verbally.

The monster rushed the warriors again. This time, its focus is on Algar. As soon as the monster grew near to Algar, he threw his spear straight through the creature's chest. He looked at Holden and raised his hand in the arm, signaling to Holden to fire his bow on the creature. Holden was able to keep the creature at bay as Algar grabbed his spear and jumped backward.

The Devil's Bandits had hundreds of strategies and tactics for combat, but none of them worked in this situation. They were all screwed. Cenric rushed forward with his Warhammer and smashed through the jaw of the massive creature, sending it flying into the wall again. But the creature just stood up yet again. It rushed towards Holden. Holden was struggling to put an arrow in his bow. Before Holden could fire his bow, the creature's long, lengthy arms grabbed him. Tears rolled down his face. He knew he was dead. But as the creature strangled him, he grabbed his dagger from his waist and stabbed the creature deep in the heart. The creature screamed and squeezed Holden's neck harder. Holden's face began to grow into a purple balloon. And with the creature's final strength, it squeezed so hard that Holden's head exploded, sending shards of his skull and brains flying everywhere. Everyone in that room began to scream.

Out of anger, Cenric charged the creature, hitting the handle of the dagger deeper into the heart of the creature. Kaito followed through, slicing all of the legs off of the creature, leaving the body sitting there on the ground. Algar cried tears, shoving his spear into the skull of the creature. Oswald stood in the middle of the room screaming for his comrade, trying to bargain with Thornos. kenelms was helpless. He fell to the ground and began weeping over Holden's body. Screaming out the prayer of the gods, trying to bring Holden back, but it did not work.

The creature lay on the ground in defeat as the warriors tore it apart in anger. Cenric grabbed his brother's body and carried it outside. "I am sorry, brother, maybe I was too harsh on you. It should have been me." Lady Liv walked over and put her hand on Cenric's shoulder. "There is no greater pain than losing a loved one, and we will make sure to bury him properly." Lady Liv had a tear running down her cheek. Although she hardly knew Holden, he still was a great warrior for her and the king.

Oswald was next out of the building. "I knew it was a mistake, making a child join our cause." Oswald was distraught. "He fought well, and his memory will live on strongly." Kaito said, exiting the keep. As Kenelm and Algar followed behind him. Algar drug the remains of the creature behind him. "I want to give this to our masters. They need to research such a creature." Algar said with tears still running down his face. All the warriors were distraught. Nobody expected to leave victorious. Even if it was a great victory for the realm, it didn't feel like one, and they had just lost a great warrior. A child, a brother, and a Devil's Bandit

The Forgotten City

By daybreak, King Dueani made it back home. "We must send our men to Frost Fall immediately," King Dueani said to his war commander.

"If we send our men to Frost Fall, it leaves our kingdom open to attack," the war commander said.

"And who has the power to attack us? NOBODY!" he shouted with a piece of the mystery meat King Bjarne gave him.

"With all due respect, your grace—" the Hand of the King started.

"I don't give a damn about your advice. Send our men to Frost Fall now!" The King shouted with food in his mouth.

"I feel really funny," King Dueani said as his throat began to swell. He fell off the throne onto the ground and began shaking uncontrollably.

"Someone get him help!" shouted the Hand. His eyes began to bleed. His face began to sink in, and his throat swelled shut. He died within minutes, a slow and painful death. The men who worked under the king scrambled for answers. But there was no evidence to be found anywhere.

A council meeting was held in the war room of the castle. "I believe we should send our men to Frost Fall," the war commander said, being the first to break the silence around the table.

"I don't believe that is in our greatest interest at this very moment!" shouted the Master of the Council.

"If we do not send our men to Frost Fall, King Bjarne may be taking our heads as well," the Hand said.

A doctor ran into the room. "My Lords! We found the cause of King Dueani's death!" the doctor shouted.

"Well, what was it?" asked the Hand of the now-dead king.

"It was a mix of deadly nightshade and henbane Datura. Both only grow in Dragons Rest," the doctor said, looking over at the Hand as he grew more and more frustrated.

"We sail to Dragons Rest now. Half our men go to Frost Fall. I am going to end this!" the Hand shouted. He was furious that not only the princesses but also the heirs of the throne and the king were all dead.

"My Lord, this is not a bright idea. You will suffer the same fate as Sun Crest, or even worse," the doctor said.

"No, I will sail with my men directly to Frost Fall. You must go to Dragons Rest alone," the war commander said as he walked out of the room, angered.

At the barracks of The Forgotten City, the war commander prepared his men for battle, but these men were different from the mercenaries. These were well-trained men, not afraid of a single thing, never backing down from a single enemy.

"My men, my noble warriors, tonight we ride into battle. The once powerful kingdom of Frost Fall must fall to our people! We must reign supreme over the realm of Nastomar!" the men all screamed in unison, smacking their swords against their shields, stomping their feet in excitement for battle.

The war commander walked his men to the docks right at the same time the Hand of the now-dead king was walking towards his boat.

"It was an honor to serve the king alongside you, Tomas," the war commander said.

"It was a great honor to fight alongside you, Reiner," Tomas said as he bid his fellow man farewell.

"This will be a cold battle. The winters have already started in Frost Fall. All of your lives are in my hands now, and it is not too late to save yourselves from this battle," Reiner tried to explain.

"We could all very well die across the seas, away from our home… Frost Fall is currently the second strongest empire in all of Nastomar, we must give this fight our all, or we all die weak men, living the shittiest of lives," Reiner feared for his own life. But he knew he had no choice. If the Hand had been unsuccessful in his battle against King Bjarne, then they would have had no choice but to win this war.

"It is a lose-lose situation. Either we die fighting, or we lose by being cowardly men rotting in the keep of our kingdom without a king," Reiner said as the boat sailed away.

Frost Fall

In Frost Fall, Cassius brought along an army of ghosts, their souls oozing on the fact that they could get revenge in some way, shape, or form. "Your grace, It is with great honor that I bring you the lost souls of Sun Crest," Cassius said, sitting at the edge of the docks awaiting his battle.

"Where did you get these men?" Asked the king.

"Your grace, I am sorry, but that does not pertain to you. What matters is that my army of ghosts will protect you and your Great noble servants from death and destruction." Cassius grew angry with the king.

"I don't even know who you are. You just show up at my gates and demand to defend my people from death. That's a very bold claim!" The king said.

"Do you want your kingdom to fall? Do you want King Bjarne to take reign over all of Nastomar?!" Cassius yelled at the king.

Cassius had no cares for the hierarchy or how kings became kings. He had no care in the world for that. He knew who the one king was. And he was forever going to follow that king. His long-lived king was Kaito Harayuma.

"Do you want the damn help or not?!" Cassius shouted again.

"Well- I mean- yes... I guess," said the king, turning around towards the gates, feeling threatened by Cassius.

"He isn't coming..." Cassius said to his army of ghosts, "King Bjarne will not be at the battlefield. He has a more important matter to attend to," Cassius said, squeezing his hands into fists so hard that his nails dug into his palms, and they began to bleed.

The ghosts moaned and groaned loudly. So loudly, some say their moans were heard across the Sea of the Dragon, in the Forgotten City, and Mystria, but nobody can truly confirm that claim.

As tension grew in Frost Fall, Cassius spoke to his army of ghosts. "Great people of the Grand Island of Sun Crest, we must send out patrols around the walls, protecting the two docks. The rest of you must begin preparing yourselves for the battle to come!" Cassius's voice echoed across the cold kingdom of Frost Fall.

Cassius, on the other hand, had remained an enigma to the king and his court. The mysterious man's motives remained unclear, and his allegiance to the absent King Kaito Harayuma raised eyebrows among the noble servants.

The king, desperate to protect his people, reluctantly accepted Cassius' assistance but kept a wary eye on the spectral army. It was sunrise of the next day, and rumors had spread like wildfire through the kingdom of Frost Fall. The townsfolk spoke in hushed tones about the impending war, questioning if there truly was an army of ghosts outside their walls. Although some were glad that Cassius had come to the rescue, many others believed he was a demon in disguise who only brought chaos and bloodshed to the kingdom of Frost Fall. Nonetheless, everyone was scared for the lives of themselves, their loved ones, and their fellow noblemen.

Cassius spent his time at the docks, overlooking the sea and awaiting the arrival of the rival army led by Reiner, the war commander from the Forgotten City. The air buzzed with anticipation, and Frost Fall prepared for the inevitable clash.

"What are we going to do about this so-called war coming to our walls?" asked war general Sir Alaric.

"I believe we let them protect us. We truly have no other chance," said the king.

"If we do not fight in this battle, our servants will consider us cowards," said the king's hand, Lady Kelbert.

"I think it is quite the opposite. From what I have gathered from our servants, most of them believe the army of ghosts could be our saving grace," said the prince, barging into the small council room.

"They are here," he said, looking at the king. "If they breach the walls, we have no choice but to fight. Ready your men inside the walls and put the kingdom on lockdown as soon as possible!" the king declared a lockdown, and the bells rang out. Everyone scurried and hid inside at once.

The kingdom of Frost Fall descended into an eerie silence as the bells echoed through the cold air, signaling the impending lockdown. The townsfolk hurriedly retreated to their homes, locking doors and shuttering windows. The spectral army, led by Cassius, patrolled the walls with an otherworldly determination.

"They are here..." Cassius said.

On the other side of the impending clash, Reiner and his army from the Forgotten City approached with calculated precision. The war commander, a stoic and battle-hardened leader, surveyed the looming fortress of Frost Fall. His soldiers, disciplined and resolute, awaited orders with a quiet intensity. The sun climbed higher and higher in the sky, casting a long shadow on the battlefield in front of Reiner's army. The tension had reached an all-time peak.

Cassius was standing in front of the spectral army, staring at the ships as they sailed closer and closer to the docks, with a very stern expression on his face. The ghosts stood behind Cassius, with their ethereal forces swirling about around them. With a cold energy, they prepared for their final battle.

Still on the sea, Reiner gave his pre-war speech. "It seems as if this kingdom has some sort of mysterious warrior fighting for it! But that means nothing to us. Nobody will crush the enemy between our fingers like we have every enemy that fought against us!" Reiner was a very cunning man, very naive but cunning. This small speech got his men amped and psyched up for the battle. Warriors rushed around the ship, equipping themselves with armor, bows, sabers, scythes, sickles, you name it. The warriors had it.

Cassius allowed the ships to dock at the docks and unload their men. As Reiner's forces disembarked from their ships, a palpable tension hung in the air. The clash of steel, the distant moans of the spectral army, and the howling wind created an atmosphere of impending doom. Reiner, with his war-hardened eyes, surveyed the spectral army and scoffed at the apparent supernatural protection of Frost Fall.

"What is this, a goddamn graveyard?" Reiner chuckled to himself.

Cassius, standing resolute at the forefront of the spectral army, felt the weight of the impending battle. His eyes locked onto Reiner, a formidable opponent whose confidence seemed unshaken. The ghosts behind Cassius swirled with cold energy, ready to unleash their ethereal powers upon the mortal intruders. The clanging of metal echoed through the walls, planting fear into the hearts of all the noble citizens.

The king and his council watched this war unfold from on top of the walls surrounding the city. The townsfolk were all still tucked away inside their homes, protected by the walls of the town. The Prince stood right at the gate, armored and ready. He gave a worrisome look to the noble guards that backed him up.

"Come out, Reiner!" Cassius, fueled by an otherworldly determination, faced Reiner on the battlefield. The clash of their weapons echoed through the air, each strike carrying the weight of vengeance and destiny. The ghosts, under Cassius's command, fought with an ethereal prowess that surpassed the mortal limits of their adversaries.

Meanwhile, Reiner's forces struggled against the relentless onslaught of the spectral army. The ethereal warriors moved with an unnatural grace, their attacks guided by an unseen force. The mortal soldiers, overwhelmed and terrified, faltered under the spectral onslaught. Cassius and Reiner met face-to-face for the very final time.

"I truly hate to say this, Reiner, but you will not be making it back home in time to choose a new king," Cassius said.

"And how do you know that for certain?" Renier asked, chuckling to himself as he cleaned his sword on the cloth near the bottom of his chest plate.

"May Thronos bring you happiness," Cassius said before pulling his sword out from its sheathe. Both the men locked eyes before Cassius lunged forward with unrelenting speed. The dance of life or death had just begun. Only one would win the prize of life, and the other, death.

The air crackled with otherworldly energy as their swords met each other for the first time. The sound of the metal clashing echoed for a moment.

"I have been watching you, Reiner. If you think you will make it out alive, you are very wrong," Cassius said before taking a large step back away from Reiner.

"I know where you were when King Dueani died. In fact, I know you did nothing to stop the poison," Cassius said, standing still waiting for Reiner to strike.

"You know nothing about anything," Renier said, lunging forward to Cassius. Cassius moved with the grace of a god, moving out of the way narrowly every time Reiner swung.

"But you're wrong. I know everything about everyone," Cassius said with a demonic grin on his face. Reiner grew more pissed off every time Cassius opened his mouth.

"Your mouth will be the death of you. I hope you remember that," Reiner said.

"You are the one who knows nothing about anyone," Cassius said as he ran forward towards Reiner. With every step Cassius took, Reiner took another step backward. Reiner realized what Cassius was trying to do. He was trying to get him as close to the edge of the dock as possible, but Reiner wouldn't let that happen so easily.

Reiner ran forward and tackled Cassius. "You seriously thought that pushing me
to the edge would work?" Reiner scoffed. "That was a very pathetic attempt, you know." Reiner said, keeping Cassius pinned to the ground. Cassius said nothing; he grinned and closed his eyes. Four massive tentacles grew out of his stomach, each one impaling Reiner in a different spot. One in both hips, one in the crotch, and one in the stomach. "I know everything about everything, and you just proved that point," Cassius said as he dangled Reiner with his tentacles. "You won't survive much longer," Reiner moaned out in pain.

As Cassius held the wounded and impaled Reiner with his tentacles, a grim satisfaction flickered in his eyes. The clash of their destinies reached its fateful conclusion on the edge of the docks, the sea witnessing the demise of the war commander from the Forgotten City.

The townsfolk, hidden within the walls, felt the vibrations of the battle. The clanging of steel and the unearthly moans of the spectral army painted a vivid picture of the struggle outside. The prince, standing armored at the gate, witnessed the supernatural display of power unleashed by Cassius.

On the walls, the king observed the events with a mix of horror and awe. The sight of Cassius's tentacles tearing into Reiner was both mesmerizing and terrifying. The prince, catching the gaze of the king, felt a chill run down his spine as the ethereal display unfolded.

As Reiner's life force faded, Cassius turned his gaze towards the king on the walls. The enigmatic protector approached, the ghostly figures of Sun Crest surrounding him in a haunting dance right before they faded away.

"What in all the gods was that?" the king shouted out in absolute terror and shock at what had just unfolded in front of him.

"I am a noble servant of the king of desolation. End times are upon us," Cassius said as he slowly walked away.

"What in the gods does that mean?" the prince shouted out.

"It means every single one of us will be dead in less than a year," Cassius declared. "I would seek Kaito Harayuma's help. He is the one who knows the way." Cassius walked far enough away from the people and disappeared into a thin plume of dark smoke like he had done countless times.

The Kaito Harayuma Empire

In the war room of Kaito's empire sat both the war commander of Dragon's Rest, Lyron Blackthorn, and his brother, the hand of King Bjarne, Eric Blackthorn. Aislinn sat at the table with Aleron, Oswald, Kenelm, Cenric, and Algar and also sat next to Lady Liv. Even the oldest sister of the FireSong family, Seraphina, made it to the meeting.

"Thank you all for gathering in this lovely empire. I see some familiar faces and some not-so-familiar faces here," Kaito says, standing up from his chair. "I have called you all here today to discuss my next step in domination. While I am sure you all know me very well, one thing some may not know is that my soon-to-be queen is pregnant with my baby."

"Congratulations, sire. I am sure you two will make for wonderful parents," Eric said as he stood from his chair to speak out.

"I am under the impression that you and your brother are the only remaining council for the new king of Dragon's Rest?" Lady Liv asked.

"Yes, my Lady, he did end up killing nearly all of his servants," Lyron said, standing himself up.

"And how do you feel about the murders of these people?" asked Oswald, grinning from ear to ear and trying to create unnecessary tension at the table.

"Why, my Lord, he is our king, and we must follow him with his every decision," Eric said.

"Your king is a disgrace to the whole realm of Nastomar, and he must be stopped before he kills us all," Algar said quickly, throwing himself out of his chair.

"Whether you are with us or not, your king will die in a month," Kaito said, knocking over the Dragon's Rest sigil on the table map.

"We came to seek peace between the kingdoms, not murder," Lyron said.

"You will either comply, or we will sink your ship before it even makes it back to Dragon's Rest," Aislinn said.

"And with what god-like power could sink a ship at sea? You have two warships to your name, and that's it," Eric said, angered that Kaito wanted King Bjarne dead.

"Two ships is enough. Now, do you want to hear the plan, or do you want to leave?" Lady Liv said.

"We will hear your plan, my Lady. I cannot say I will like it, but I shall hear you out," Lyron said, bowing his head to the future queen.

"Good, now pay attention," Oswald said, pointing over to Kaito.

"First things first, the venue is being held in Ember Fall, my original home, and the place his father eradicated the good men, women, and children that lived there. Aislinn, you must go to Mystria. Queen Saga made a special type of paralyzing poison. Once you retrieve it, you must go to Ember Fall…"

"Aye, aye, your grace," Aislinn said.

"And Aleron, you must stay with me in my kingdom. I want to meet this dragon that hatched," Kaito said, looking with adoration at the young child who fought courageously.

"Wait, did I hear that correctly? Do you have a dragon?" Eric was horrified. He had never heard such a thing as a dragon being domesticated.

"Like the fire-breathing monsters that burn down entire kingdoms?" Lyron was almost as shocked as his brother, but he had also heard the rumor that the dragon of the sea had killed thousands of men outside of the walls.

"Not necessarily. This dragon is just a baby, and it doesn't seem to possess any fire-breathing capabilities," Aislinn said, eager to help kill the Human Butcher.

"The third step in this plan is on you two. You will go back to Dragon's Rest with this note. It reads, 'Your grace, King Bjarne of Dragon's Rest, you are invited to Ember Fall for the grand wedding of two powerful houses. We invite you on the terms of peace and tranquility for all the lands in the realm of Nastomar.' You must convince King Bjarne to come in peace alone and drink from our glasses of wine," Kaito said, hoping that these men who sat around him would be loyal to the soon-to-be immortal king of Nastomar.

"Your grace, what if he sees through the letter and decides not to come?" asked Lyron.

"If all should fail and he denies our invitation, you must kill him yourself-" Kaito started to say before the door to the room swung open.

"He won't deny. He wants his life to be ended, and you, Kaito, must do this in the most painful way imaginable," Cassius hung in the doorway of the room.

"I'm sorry, Cassius. How do you know this?" asked Kenelm, laughing.

"I am everywhere all at once. There is not a single thing I do not know," Cassius began saying.

"If that's true, tell me what I did to join the Devil's Bandits." Kenelm knew only the members of the Devil's Bandits knew this information.

"That is easy enough, Kenelm. Your true identity is Kenelm Chadwicke. You are the only bastard son of the Chadwicke bloodline. When your father bastardized you and gave your sister the title of Lady of Winter Crest, you went berserk, shooting your father. At the same time, he was most vulnerable taking a shit, and you stabbed your eight-year-old sister in cold blood with a scalpel from your mother's in-home medical center. As you ran from your mistakes, you met Oswald, who was three years older than you. He took you under his wing, introducing you to what is now known as the Devil's Bandits." As Cassius says, he has been around for all of eternity; he has seen everything everyone has done.

"By the gods, that was spot on! Even down to the age of my sister." Kenelm was shocked to see anyone who knew about his troubling past. "I also know that you killed three guards on your way to the meeting location in the city with Oswald."

"Now, getting back to the plan, if anything fails, you must stop him at all costs," Kaito said, pushing a Dark Steel dagger across the table.

"This is what you shall kill him with," Algar said, chuckling to himself.

"If all goes according to plan, and he does meet us in Ember Fall, Lady Liv will be the one to finish him off. After all the stress he had put on Lady Liv and me, it was time for her to finish it once and for all. We show no mercy to our enemies, and this time is no different," Kaito said.

"Devil's Bandits, you must go to Ember Fall and meet with the FireSongs. They will guide you in how the venue will be built, and you must help them," Kaito said, pointing towards Ember Fall on the table map.

"Now, we must all go our separate ways. You all know your part in this plan, so carry this out correctly, and I will make sure you all have a special job in my council," Kaito said as everyone got up and filed out the door and into the courtyard one by one. Lyron and Eric were the last two to stand in the courtyard. They stood close to one another.

"Are we sure he can be trusted?" asked Lyron.

"He is our only chance to escape. If he hadn't invited us, we would have been forever trapped in the council," Eric said. "Look, we have to do what Kaito said. If there is any chance this could work, we will forever be in Kaito's debt," Eric said, picking at the skin on his thumb.

"Well, if it works, who will take over? Ask the king of Dragon's Rest?" Lyron asked. Lyron wasn't the smartest when it came to how knighting and becoming a king worked, so he was extra serious about this question.

"Kaito would most likely become king, but he would probably appoint someone to take over for Dragon's Rest."

"We must go. Our time here has come to an end. It is about time we get this wicked man killed," Eric says as he walks towards the docks.

"Next time we see each other, I will have the key ingredient to killing our worst nightmare," Aislinn jokingly said as she hugged Kaito goodbye.

"You know, you're more of a dad to me than my real father ever was," Aislinn said as she got on top of a massive horse.

"I know, my child. Now go. Queen Saga awaits your arrival," Kaito and Liv walked hand in hand.

"It seems as if we will be on top of the world soon enough, your grace," Lady Liv said.

"Yes, but at what cost?" Kaito said. "I have slaughtered thousands of men in only a few months, all to get this chance," Kaito said.

"Even if you are second-guessing, you must look on the bright side. Soon, you will have a queen and a child, and you will have gotten revenge on the people who got you into this mess," Lady Liv said happily.

"My princess, we will reign the realm of Nastomar together, and when our baby is old enough, he will take the realm from us. The once-dead bloodline will reign once again," Kaito said, putting his hand on the princess's stomach, feeling the unborn baby's kicks. "We must meet with Aleron in the crypt. He has something important to show us," Kaito said, eager to meet the dragon.

"Do you think the dragon story we heard is true?" asked Lady Liv, concerned that the egg was a hoax and no dragon was awaiting them.

"There is no reason for Aleron and Aislinn to lie to us; that would be treason,

and I would have their tongues ripped from their mouths," Kaito said jokingly. Even in such serious times, Kaito kept a fun and caring manner. Some of his servants say he is too laid back. While others say he is just the perfect amount of caring and serious.
As Kaito and Liv approached the giant doors of the crypt, Oswald, Algar, Cenric, Kenelm, and Seraphina stood waiting for Kaito. "Your grace," they all said. "Oh, and my Lady," they all caught themselves when Lady Liv walked up a few feet away from Kaito.

"I know you wanted to see this baby dragon Aislinn and Aleron were talking about," Seraphina said, eager to go deep into the crypts and see the baby dragon. "Your grace, do you believe the rumors are true?" asked Algar, excited to hear what Kaito had to say.

"We have seen a dragon before. Remember the war against Eldandoor? The massive dragon of the sea torched at least three thousand men," Oswald said, smacking Algar upside the head.

"I guess there is only one way to find out," Cenric said, opening the doors to the crypt. "It is pretty dark down there. Are you sure Aleron is down there?" Kenelm said having an irrational fear of the dark since he was a young boy due to the midnight murders happening in his town.

"I'm sure Aleron wouldn't stand us up. Aislinn would have his head for such a thing," Lady Liv said, giggling to herself as she took the first steps into the crypt. This was no usual crypt, and this was the secondary crypt only used to keep prisoners of war, even though so far, the Kaito Harayuma Empire had only taken two prisoners who both died at the hands of Kaito.

The venture into the crypt took a few minutes, and the walls were close to one another, leaving only room for one person at a time to go. Lady Liv was the only one who held a torch, and so after she got to the bottom of the long skinny walkway, there was a dim light at the bottom, which was the only light leading Kaito and his friends down to the bottom of the crypt. Even after everyone made it to the bottom of the crypt's stairway, they had quite a ways to go til they reached Aleron. And when they finally did, there was a dim light, no torch, no nothing.

"Blow your torch out, my Lady," Aleron said, "Look at her glow. The masters believe she's a special type of dragon." Aleron was excited to show off Inessa.

"Does she have a name yet?" asked Kaito.

"I believe Aislinn named her Inessa, and she told me it means pure or clean. I quite like it," Aleron laid his only hand on the back of the four-foot-long dragon.

Algar put his hand out, preparing to touch the dragon. "The first time you touch her, you might feel a little shock. Her scales hold electricity; we learned she could be another way of powering things around the town. But the masters say it would take years of work before we could do it." Aleron warned Algar of what was about to happen and shared a neat insight about the dragon.

Everyone was in shock when Inessa let Algar touch her. "This is mad, and I have my hands resting on a dragon!" Algar was so excited he couldn't even express it properly.

"Oswald! Put your hand on her. The feeling is unreal!" shouted Algar, taking his hand away from the dragon. Oswald reached down and touched the back of the dragon, although this time, the dragon decided to shock Oswald a little bit harder, sending his hair sticking right up. "This is mad! I feel like I'm on top of the world just touching this creature!"

Everyone took turns touching Inessa, but Kaito wanted a moment with just Aleron and Lady Liv in the room. "My Lords and my Lady, can you leave me and Aleron to the room," Kaito said, dismissing everyone from the room so that the king and princess could have a moment alone with the creature.

Everyone walked away from the crypt, slowly starting their journey to the places they needed to be to help with the plan. "Your grace, if I may ask, what is your plan with the dragon?" asked Aleron.

"Well, my child, it was staying in the crypts until I took control of Nastomar. Afterward, we will use it as our biggest defense to scare away any rebellions or people who stand against me and Lady Liv," Kaito said happily, explaining the situation.

"How big do the masters say it will be?" asked Lady Liv.

"It all depends on what it is fed and where it is kept," Aleron explained.

"We shall make room for it in ember fall then," Lady Liv said, overruling the king's ruling. This didn't upset Kaito; it made him quite happy to see that Lady Liv could still think for herself without Kaito having to make every ruling and do everything himself.

"We must get going. We don't have much longer until it is time for our wedding," Kaito said as he walked away from Inessa.

"Thank you for your time, your grace," Aleron said as Lady Liv and Kaito walked away.

As they walked out of the crypt, they began to speak about life. "You know, Kaito, ever since you saved me from Eldandoor, I have been grateful for you. I used to hate you. I thought to myself that I would never marry you and that I would never be the mother of your child, but now that I have fought alongside you, now that I have gotten to know you. I think I do love you. I know I have never said those three words, mostly because it has been difficult to say them but also because I have been afraid to say them. Just know I am happy to be your queen and

the mother to our soon-to-be-born child."
Queen Liv had grown to love her king truly;
she was truly loyal to his cause and was fully
prepared to do anything she had to do to
remain loyal to her one true king.

"I am happy to be the one to have
rescued you. Ever since I rescued you, I have
had a genuine purpose and a person to come
home to at the end of the day. I truly love
you, too," Kaito said right before he went in
to kiss his soon-to-be wife. The journey to
this point has been long and dreadful, but
now it is finally looking up for the Harayuma
family. Kaito might gain his immortality
sooner than he thought. But at what cost
would he gain this power? A lot was riding
on his noble servants. If a single thing goes
wrong, the world of Nastomar could fall to a
wretched and evil man. A man who cares
about nothing more than power. This man
had killed children. Innocent citizens, dogs,
cats, pregnant women, and the elderly. Even
his brother and father died at his hands,
which would be forever stained red.

Dragons Rest

The council had just headed towards Dragon's Rest, while Tomas, on the other hand, had just arrived. Tomas was a tall man, and he wasn't very experienced in combat, but he had fought a few times with King Dueani when he was still in power. He was furious with King Bjarne for the murder of King Dueani, his only friend and his king. Tomas marched through the desolate streets of Dragon's Rest, the echoes of his footsteps mingling with the eerie tones of a city scarred by recent war. The once bustling marketplace now lay in ruins, its stalls reduced to ashes, and the air carried the acrid scent of smoldering debris. Broken windows whispered tales of violence, and shadows danced among the skeletal remains of buildings. The people Tomas did see, however, hid away as soon as they saw him. The people of Dragon's Rest lived in such fear after the battle King Bjarne had made.

Tomas had his eyes set on killing Bjarne, and his heart was filled with hatred and grief. Tomas scanned the wreckage of Dragon's Rest, looking for any sign of his enemy, King Bjarne, also known as the human butcher or the king killer. Charred remnants of humans and homes still littered the streets of Dragon's Rest. "Will this place ever see its former glory?" Tomas mumbled to himself, kicking a charred ribcage away from his feet.

Tomas took a moment, clenching his fists at the sight of the destroyed castle. He recalled all the moments he had lived out with King Dueani, who was like a father figure to Tomas more than he was the king. Tomas didn't just think of King Dueani's happiest moments. He recalled the countless wars and battles King Dueani fought through. He thought of the mercenary band King Dueani paid for just for his two children. The closer Tomas got to the castle, the closer the council came to the docks of Dragon's Rest. It was a battle between speed, who could make it to King Bjarne faster, the council, who was sailing from a distant land, or Tomas, a revenge-seeking young man set on killing a king. A king that had almost a million deaths on his hands.

As Tomas put his right foot forward to touch the first step of the remains of the castle, a group of guards caught him. A child pointed his finger towards Tomas and said, "He has a weapon." The three guards ran forward toward Tomas. Tomas pulled his sword out of its sheath and got into an offensive stance. "Remember what King Dueani taught you," Tomas mumbled to himself. The first guard ran towards Tomas. Tomas began charging towards him, his sword pushed directly in front of him, aimed for the guard's stomach. Then suddenly, Tomas felt the tip of his sword get heavier. The sword dug directly into the stomach of the guard. Tomas was shocked. He dug the sword deeper, then ripped it out. The guard's armor made a loud noise as his lifeless body hit the ground. "Which one of you is next?!" Tomas shouted at the two guards who stood in his way to revenge. The guards shared a look, and both ran towards Tomas. The first guard swung for Tomas's head. Tomas ducked instinctively. When he peeked up from ducking, the other guard was in his vicinity. Tomas slashed his sword towards the right hip of the guard. And with such force, it penetrated through the armor, cutting deep into the ribs. He tried to push the sword through even more but couldn't. Tomas pulled the sword out and turned around to the final guard. Tomas felt his first-ever feeling of bloodlust and true battle adrenaline. Tomas swung for the other man, knocking the helmet off the guard's head and knocking the guard to the ground.

"Spare me, please, I beg by the gods, please!" the guard pleaded for his life. "You serve the wrong man… May Thornos bring you happiness?" Tomas lifted his sword and swiftly dragged it into the guard's head. And as he pulled the sword out, chunks of the guard's brain sat on the sword.

Meanwhile, the council was nearly at the Dragon's Rest docks. "We will dock before the hour of the dark," one of the sailors said to Eric. Every step Tomas took towards the throne room was another foot. The massive warship got closer to Dragon's Rest. Tomas wiped the blood and chunks of brain from his sword on one of the dead guard's cloth undershirts. The metallic tang of the blood hung in the air, and the taste laid deep into Tomas's mouth. The encounter with those guards reminded Tomas that humans, believe it or not, are still mortal. Any single human could die at any single second.

Tomas ascended the castle steps one by one. As the warship sailed closer to Dragon's Rest inch by inch, the memories of King Dueani still sat in Tomas's head, growing stronger by the second. As Tomas reached the doors to the castle, the council of Lyron and Eric reached the docks of Dragon's Rest. Unbeknownst to Tomas, the council took their first step off of the warship and onto the dry land of Dragon's Rest. Tomas had finally reached the top of the castle, to the room in which King Bjarne's throne sat. Tomas kicked the door open and barged in. "Are you ready to die, Bjarne?!" Tomas shouted. "Who the hell even are you?" King Bjarne shouted out as he stood up from his throne. "My name is Tomas, and I am the hand of King Dueani," Tomas said in an angered yet calm tone. "He's dead, I killed him myself," King Bjarne scoffed, laughing at the fact that someone had the nerve to come to Dragon's Rest over a king who had a pathetic reign. "I am here to kill you. Draw your sword." Tomas knew he stood no chance, and it was a shot in the dark and suicide for him to even think of fighting the human butcher. "If you wish to die, I will make sure it is slow and painful," King Bjarne said as he grabbed his sword from beside his throne. The sword was stained with the blood of his enemies, and this fact struck fear into Tomas's soul. Tomas lunged forward, leaping into death's jaws. Bjarne already had the upper hand; he knew the land, and Tomas didn't. Bjarne moved out of the way of Tomas's attack just in the nick of time, sending Tomas to the throne. "Given up so soon?" Bjarne said, taunting his new prey. "Not quite." Tomas scoffed as he threw himself to his feet and put his back towards the door out of the throne room. The throne room door swung open, and Eric saw Tomas and Bjarne in combat. Eric knew he had to kill the man who was fighting the king he was about to lie to if he wanted to keep his cover. Eric walked up behind Tomas and grabbed him by his silky hair. Bjarne walked up to Tomas. "How does it feel to die pretending to live a happy life?" Bjarne asked, laughing at Tomas's futile attempt to kill him. Tomas spat in King Bjarne's face. This angered King Bjarne enough to slit his throat slowly. The blood leaked out from right behind the sword that slit his throat. "Now, my boys, welcome home!" King Bjarne said, wiping his sword on the cloth shirt that Tomas wore. "We must speak, your grace," Lyron said as he approached the king with the letter in his hand. "What's this?" King Bjarne asked. "Read it, your grace. It is of uttermost importance," Eric said as he stood towards the back of the room, far away from the king. "So they call peace?" Bjarne asks Lyron. "Yes, your grace, that letter came from the hands of Kaito himself," Lyron responds. "Only under the condition that you go to their wedding," Eric explains. "Must I go alone? I cannot even bring a knight?" Bjarne was confused and concerned that they wanted only him to go. "Your grace, it is only a day outing. I'm sure Kaito will put you in great care," Lyron says, trying to keep his calm. "I will go, but rest assured, I will carve the unborn babe from her stomach, and I will feed it to every one of my servants here." Bjarne was a quick-witted man; he knew exactly what to say, and he had no control over when it came out of his mouth. He didn't care about what he said because he was the king. After all, who was going to stop him from saying such atrocious things? "As you wish, your grace, we will ready the ship tomorrow," Eric said as he and Lyron filed out of the throne room to their respective chambers. "Have you gone mad?!" Lyron whispered, trying to make sure nobody could overhear their conversation. "You did not have to help Bjarne. We could have helped that man kill him." "We would have failed, and you know that. Even if there were three of us, he's stronger," Eric whispered, even though he was extremely annoyed. "Plus, Kaito wants to be the one who has his head. If we had taken it from him, don't you think he would have been angered?" Eric was annoyed trying to get rest from his long journey back home. "I suppose you are correct, but even still, I have a sinking suspicion about Kaito. Something is up with him, but I just can't get a finger on what it is." Lyron fell backward

into his bed, ready to get his first full night's
rest in a week

Mystria

Aislinn rode into Mystria, being
greeted by all the townsfolk. Aislinn had
grown quite a reputation in the south for
killing one of the Dueani twins, being one of
the youngest members of Kaito's council, and
becoming the youngest knight to ever be in
the realm of Nastomar.

"My Lady, may I interest you in a
meal?" asked one of the noble servants as
Aislinn rode through the market square.

"I am alright, thank you, though,"
Aislinn said, holding a smile from ear to ear.
Mystria had grown since the battle against
Eldandoor. After walking through the streets
of Mystira for a while, Aislinn finally decided

to see Queen Saga and her council, who were waiting patiently for her.

As Aislinn walked through the doors into the council room, she overheard talk of Queen Saga bending the knee to Kaito, something Kaito had been hoping for since the start of his reign.

"Hello, sir, Aislinn of Frost Fall. That is the correct term for you now, right?" asked Queen Saga with a look of excitement to finally interact with Aislinn.

"Yes, your grace, Kaito Knighted me a while back, a while after my dragon had hatched."

"Yes, I have heard wonderful things about this baby dragon. Its name is Inessa, right?" Queen Saga was not able to bear children, so she felt a connection to Aislinn. She saw a fearsome warrior deep inside her.

"Yes, your grace, Inessa is a special type of dragon like no other." Aislinn was nervous; she could tell a lot stood on the line with this first impression.

"Now, I am almost positive you are here for the Hemlock Kaito asked for." Queen Saga didn't know the plan completely, and she was curious to know it. "Why don't you stay a while? We can have a nice chat while my hand gathers the poison for you!" Queen Saga was nervous, too, although you could hardly tell.

"Your grace, is it true that you used to have some sort of magic within you?" Aislinn asked curiously.

"Yes, my dear, right under this room is the chapel to a large underground church. I would love to show you sometime. However, today is not a great time for such a thing." Queen Saga grew a little sad in these moments. "I am surrendering my title as Queen of Mystria. I will be giving my throne and crown to Kaito. He deserves to rule the kingdoms. I hardly know the young man, but I am sure he will make a fine king as he has already." Queen Saga knew the end of their reign was coming. She was glad it was ending in a great, honorable way. "Tell me, if Kaito was to take you as his daughter, would you accept?" Queen Saga was asked to ask this question to see what sort of response she was given.

"I would your grace, but I don't believe our king would ever ask such a thing." Aislinn said quickly, confused about why she would bring up such a topic.

"I believe he would, given the circumstances. You fought alongside him multiple times, and you have saved the princess multiple times as well. You truly deserve it." Queen Saga was handed a punch with a purple vial in it. "Slip this in your opponent's wine, and he will become paralyzed from the waist down, causing him a great amount of discomfort." Queen Saga said, placing the pouch in Aislinn's hand. "Now, you must ride to Ember Fall; they are all awaiting you."

"I do not wish to leave just yet. May I stay a little while longer, your grace?" Aislinn was finally content with where she was in life, but she wanted to know more about Queen Saga. "Tell me, your grace, are you originally from Mystria?" Aislinn asked, curious about Queen Saga's backstory.

"When I was just a young girl, Mystria had just begun to form. It was once a land of noble farmers seeking refuge away from Eldandoor. My family escaped Eldandoor right after I was born. That kingdom was no place for such a child like me. My family helped build this castle. I know it like the back of my hand. When I was young, around your age. I met the king. Lord Samuel Saga. He was a fine young Lord. Great in combat, even better in bed. Samuel was not king yet, but his grandfather was. He was a real cranky old man, always screaming at the maids. Refusing to bathe and eat. That was eventually his downfall. He starved to death with a large table of food right in front of him, and then Lord Samuel's father came to inherit the throne. He was a great man. He survived quite a while, only to go off and die in the war against the dead city. A true fool's mistake. Samuel was the greatest king Mystria had ever seen. He is the reason we have the mystical forces here in the kingdom. He built the church below us, and his council was used to try to get closer to our great god, Thornos. However, that endeavor was his downfall. He was possessed by an archdemon and had to be killed, and his body is forever locked in the crypt below that church. Nobody is allowed in, and nobody is allowed out. We had no children, and I could never give him one, even though I tried countless times. He gave the throne to me, and here I have sat ever since. It has been about ten years. And I believe it's time a young king takes over for me."

"So that's why you want Kaito to take it? Because you have grown tired of the crown." Aislinn asked.

"No, Not for that reason, but for the reason that I know he will reign supreme. A wise man came to me a while ago and explained what was about to happen. I believe every word he said. No man would lie about such things."

"And what was this wise old man's name, My queen?"

"His name was Cassius, the hand of Thornos himself. And he had facts to prove it." Aislinn's facial expression grew cold, and she said, "I must go. Ember Fall is waiting for me." Aislinn then turned around and got on her horse. Terrified of what she had just learned.

Ember Fall

Aislinn rode into a completely remodeled kingdom of Ember Fall. Although no citizens had moved into the kingdom yet, the houses were large. And the merchant square was already built. The sigils of the rock with an ember-filled center strung along the walls and homes, The large castle on top of a hill, With ember-tinted windows. And a stairway of sleek black marble. The kingdom had come quite a long way from the rubble and ash that it once was. The venue for the wedding had not yet been set up. What sat in the location the venue was supposed to be was a flat patch of black marble and ember. As Aislinn rode through the gates, Aleron and Inessa stood waiting for her. "My Lady, we have awaited your arrival for quite some time." Aleron said, helping his knight off her horse. "How was the journey?" "it was alright. I got the poison, and I got back in one piece, so that is good." Aislinn leaned in to kiss Aleron, and Inessa growled playfully. "She has grown since I last saw her." Aislinn said as the baby dragon Inessa flew beside her. "She's about four and a half feet long now." Aleron was pleased with the size of their only few-week-old baby. "What have they been feeding her?" Aislinn asked." goats, pigs, sheep, sometimes the occasional goose." Aleron chuckled to himself. "To think that I would be the father of a dragon someday would have baffled a younger me." Aleron was having a joyous time talking with Aislinn at the entrance of Ember Fall. "This is most definitely an upgrade from the last kingdom." Aislinn joked. The Kaito Harayuma empire was a bit of a pig sty with citizens everywhere, burglaries happening daily, and even a string of mysterious murders. "See that large building over there? That is Inessa's chamber. She will have room to grow to full size in there." Aleron pointed at a large building, almost looking like a coliseum. It had an ember glass roof protecting Inessa from the elements but still giving her ample amounts of sunlight. Aislinn put her head on Aleron's shoulder. "Is something the matter, my Lady?" Asked Aleron, concerned. "The time is coming, and it's almost time for the wedding." Aislinn said. "Aye, but we are currently the only people here. Kaito and Lady Liv haven't even shown up yet." Aleron said. "And the Devil's Bandits and the FireSong family? Where are they? " Aislinn asked, confused as to why nobody was in the kingdom. "The Devil's bandits went hunting, and the Firesongs are currently gathering material for the venue. They should be back shortly." "how about I show you around?" Aleron said as he moved away from Aislinn. Aislinn gathered herself and followed Aleron. But right as they began to walk away, the Firesong family arrived. They rode their massive warhorses, each carrying a cart of wood, metals, and coal on their backs. "My ladies! Welcome back to Ember Falls!" Aleron had an excited expression on his face. He was eager to learn what the FireSongs wanted them to do. "Since Kaito and Lady Liv are not here yet, and the bandits are still hunting, I'm going to need your help building the venue. It should only take until the hour of darkness to set up. The Firesongs were a family full of inventors, so the three sisters knew their stuff when it came to metalwork and carpentry. " Aleron, you must build the chairs for the venue. And Aislinn, you must help us build the large feast table for all the meat the bandits will bring back with them." Emberyln said she might have been young. But she was bossy and was the best at carpentry. For hours, Aislinn helped craft a table. The middle was made of ember with little fossils inside of it, and Aleron built chair after chair until his hands could bear it no more. After nightfall, the Firesong family sent Aislinn and Aleron to their chambers. Although they were ordered to separate chambers, Aleron snuck out late at night and lay in bed with Aislinn. When morning rolled around, there were pies, bread, soups, and plenty of meats sitting at the large table Aislinn helped build. The Devil's bandits arrived late into the night and worked hard into the morning preparing the feast. Oswald called for Aislinn. "Sir Aislinn, This pitcher right in front of you… it is marked with the sigil of Dragons Rest. Put the poison inside of it now. The poison will take a moment to mix with the wine inside. Whatever you do, do not drink from this pitcher. It will very well paralyze you." Oswald stated he said it loud enough for Aleron, Seraphian, Avalon, Emberlyn, Kenelm, Algar, and Cenric to hear. "Aye, what if I want to be stuck in a chair for the rest of my life?" Aleron jokingly said. "Why then, you can drink as much as you want, but leave some for that wicked child slayer." Oswald chuckled and mumbled under his breath, "What a hilarious boy." Later in the morning, Cassius arrived. "Ah yes, the old wise man." Kenelm said, putting his arm around Cassius, "Do not touch me. I will hurt you." Cassius was a grumpy old man. Partially because he knew what was about to unfold in front of him. And partially because he hated weddings. He was an officiary for weddings for years and years before he became who he is now. An hour later, Kaito and Lady Liv arrived, ecstatic by the look of Kaito's home. He gave Seraphina a large, long, warm hug, "You restored Ember Fall to its former beauty, something everyone in the realm said would never happen. And yet you did it, and you pulled it off!" Kaito and Lady Liv strolled the streets for hours, going from building to building and looking through all of the merchant vendors. "Kaito, do you think he will come?" asked Lady Liv. "Who? Bjarne?" asked Kaito. "I believe he will be here in the next couple of hours. Although I'm not sure if everyone is prepared yet." Kaito said. "Are you ready to kill our final enemy?" Kaito asked, gripping the sword in his hand. 'I think I can do it, and I will do this for you, my love." Lady Liv knew what Bjarne had done. He had helped his father with the planned attack on Ember Fall, and he had killed the entire island tribe of Sun Crest, children and all. "He killed King Dueani, who may not have been a great and just king, but he was still human. He even killed his father and brother for no reason. " Our wedding is tomorrow. Is there anything you'd like to do before that?" Kaito asked; he was serious. Any wish that Lady Liv could think of, they would do. "Bring everyone to the castle. I want a final feast among us." Lady Liv said, looking up at the massive Castle that towered over Ember Fall. " as you wish, my Lady." Kaito gathered everyone, and they all walked in a large group through the castle, looking inside every room at the luxurious furniture, the grand windows, and the ember-engraved throne. And the long table that sat inside the Food hall. Everyone sat down. "This will be my final meal as a Lady. Tomorrow, Kaito and I Will be King and Queen of Nastomar. For that, we sit in each other's company at this large table, with great food in front of us!" Queen Liv raised her glass in the air. "A Toast to the soon-to-be King and Queen of Nastomar!" Algar shouted out. All their glasses made of metal clanged together, and loud cheers were exchanged around the table. " so Kaito, how does it feel, having every kingdom bend the knee to you?" Aleron asked. "It Feels amazing, almost as if I am on top of the world!" Kaito exclaimed. "Aye, you went from having nothing to your name to having everything you could ever ask for, right?" Aleron said, proud of how far his king has come. "I went from having no home to having the most fancy and expensive kingdoms in Nastomar, all because of the allies I have made along the way! I would like to make a toast to my friendships and my allies alike!" once again, everyone clanked their cups together and drank more wine. Before they night it, it was nightfall again. They all knew that King Bjarne would arrive in the morning, and the wedding was the same day. Everyone went off to their chambers in the castle to get a full night's rest. Early in the morning, King Bjarne made it into the kingdom. He was amazed to see the kingdom standing once again. "How did you do this so swiftly, Kaito?" Bjarne asked as he got off his horse. "We had backing from the Nastomar bank, and we had some of the best builders assist us." Kaito explained. "It is great that we can unite our kingdoms again and get rid of the war that your father began." Kaito said, smiling. Knowing that King Bjarne would be yet another death at his feet in a few hours. Everyone met at the venue in the afternoon, sitting around the table. They feasted and drank wine. Even Bjarne drank, but he still drank Aislinn rode into a completely remodeled kingdom of Ember Fall. Although no citizens had moved into the kingdom yet, the houses were large. And the merchant square was already built. The sigils of the rock with an ember-filled center strung along the walls and homes, the large castle on top of a hill, with ember-tinted windows. And a stairway of sleek black marble. The kingdom had come quite a long way from the rubble and ash that it once was. The venue for the wedding had not yet been set up. What sat in the location the venue was supposed to be was a flat patch of black marble and ember.

As Aislinn rode through the gates, Aleron and Inessa stood waiting for her.

"My Lady, we have awaited your arrival for quite some time." Aleron said, helping his knight off her horse. "How was the journey?"

"It was alright. I got the poison, and I got back in one piece, so that is good." Aislinn leaned in to kiss Aleron, and Inessa growled playfully.

"She has grown since I last saw her." Aislinn said as the baby dragon Inessa flew beside her.

"She's about four and a half feet long now." Aleron was pleased with the size of their only few-week-old baby.

"What have they been feeding her?" Aislinn asked.

"Goats, pigs, sheep, sometimes the occasional goose." Aleron chuckled to himself. "To think that I would be the father of a dragon someday would have baffled a younger me." Aleron was having a joyous time talking with Aislinn at the entrance of Ember Fall.

"This is most definitely an upgrade from the last kingdom." Aislinn joked. The Kaito Harayuma empire was a bit of a pig sty with citizens everywhere, burglaries happening daily, and even a string of mysterious murders.

"See that large building over there? That is Inessa's chamber. She will have room to grow to full size in there." Aleron pointed at a large building, almost looking like a coliseum. It had an ember glass roof protecting Inessa from the elements but still giving her ample amounts of sunlight. Aislinn put her head on Aleron's shoulder. "Is something the matter, my Lady?" Asked Aleron, concerned.

"The time is coming, and it's almost time for the wedding." Aislinn said.

"Aye, but we are currently the only people here. Kaito and Lady Liv haven't even shown up yet." Aleron said.

"And the Devil's Bandits and the FireSong family? Where are they?" Aislinn asked, confused as to why nobody was in the kingdom.

"The Devil's bandits went hunting, and the Firesongs are currently gathering material for the venue. They should be back shortly."

"How about I show you around?" Aleron said as he moved away from Aislinn. Aislinn gathered herself and followed Aleron. But right as they began to walk away, the Firesong family arrived. They rode their massive warhorses, each carrying a cart of wood, metals, and coal on their backs.

"My ladies! Welcome back to Ember Falls!" Aleron had an excited expression on his face. He was eager to learn what the FireSongs wanted them to do.

"Since Kaito and Lady Liv are not here yet, and the bandits are still hunting, I'm going to need your help building the venue. It should only take until the hour of darkness to set up."
The Firesongs were a family full of inventors, so the three sisters knew their stuff when it came to metalwork and carpentry.

"Aleron, you must build the chairs for the venue. And Aislinn, you must help us

build the large feast table for all the meat the bandits will bring back with them."
Emberyln said she might have been young. But she was bossy and was the best at carpentry.

For hours, Aislinn helped craft a table. The middle was made of ember with little fossils inside of it, and Aleron built chair after chair until his hands could bear it no more. After nightfall, the Firesong family sent Aislinn and Aleron to their chambers. Although they were ordered to separate chambers, Aleron snuck out late at night and lay in bed with Aislinn.

When morning rolled around, there were pies, bread, soups, and plenty of meats sitting at the large table Aislinn helped build. The Devil's bandits arrived late into the night and worked hard into the morning preparing the feast.
Oswald called for Aislinn. "Sir Aislinn, This pitcher right in front of you… it is marked with the sigil of Dragons Rest. Put the poison inside of it now. The poison will take a moment to mix with the wine inside. Whatever you do, do not drink from this pitcher. It will very well paralyze you."

Oswald stated he said it loud enough for Aleron, Seraphian, Avalon, Emberlyn, Kenelm, Algar, and Cenric to hear.

"Aye, what if I want to be stuck in a chair for the rest of my life?" Aleron jokingly said.

"Why then, you can drink as much as you want, but leave some for that wicked child slayer." Oswald chuckled and mumbled under his breath, "What a hilarious boy."

Later in the morning, Cassius arrived. "Ah yes, the old wise man." Kenelm said, putting his arm around Cassius,

"Do not touch me. I will hurt you." Cassius was a grumpy old man. Partially because he knew what was about to unfold in front of him. And partially because he hated weddings. He was an officiary for weddings for years and years before he became who he is now.

An hour later, Kaito and Lady Liv arrived, ecstatic by the look of Kaito's home. He gave Seraphina a large, long, warm hug, "You restored Ember Fall to its former beauty, something everyone in the realm said would never happen. And yet you did it, and you pulled it off!" Kaito and Lady Liv strolled the streets for hours, going from building to building and looking through all of the merchant vendors.

"Kaito, do you think he will come?" asked Lady Liv.

"Who? Bjarne?" asked Kaito. "I believe he will be here in the next couple of hours. Although I'm not sure if everyone is prepared yet." Kaito said.

"Are you ready to kill our final enemy?" Kaito asked, gripping the sword in his hand.

"I think I can do it, and I will do this for you, my love." Lady Liv knew what Bjarne had done. He had helped his father with the planned attack on Ember Fall, and he had killed the entire island tribe of Sun Crest, children and all. "He killed King Dueani, who may not have been a great and just king, but he was still human. He even killed his father and brother for no reason."

"Our wedding is tomorrow. Is there anything you'd like to do before that?" Kaito asked; he was serious. Any wish that Lady Liv could think of, they would do.

"Bring everyone to the castle. I want a final feast among us." Lady Liv said, looking up at the massive Castle that towered over Ember Fall.

"As you wish, my Lady." Kaito gathered everyone, and they all walked in a large group through the castle, looking inside every room at the luxurious furniture, the grand windows, and the ember-engraved throne. And the long table that sat inside the Food hall.
Everyone sat down.

"This will be my final meal as a Lady. Tomorrow, Kaito and I Will be King and Queen of Nastomar. For that, we sit in each other's company at this large table, with great food in front of us!" Queen Liv raised her glass in the air.

"A Toast to the soon-to-be King and Queen of Nastomar!" Algar shouted out. All their glasses made of metal clanged together, and loud cheers were exchanged around the table.

"So Kaito, how does it feel, having every kingdom bend the knee to you?" Aleron asked.

"It Feels amazing, almost as if I am on top of the world!" Kaito exclaimed.

"Aye, you went from having nothing to your name to having everything you could ever ask for, right?" Aleron said, proud of how far his king has come.

"I went from having no home to having the most fancy and expensive kingdoms in Nastomar, all because of the allies I have made along the way! I would like to make a toast to my friendships and my allies alike!" once again, everyone clanked their cups together and drank more wine.

Before they knew it, it was nightfall again. They all knew that King Bjarne would arrive in the morning, and the wedding was the same day. Everyone went off to their chambers in the castle to get a full night's rest.

Early in the morning, King Bjarne made it into the kingdom. He was amazed to see the kingdom standing once again.

"How did you do this so swiftly, Kaito?" Bjarne asked as he got off his horse.

"We had backing from the Nastomar bank, and we had some of the best builders assist us." Kaito explained. "It is great that we can unite our kingdoms again and get rid of the war that your father began." Kaito said, smiling. Knowing that King Bjarne would be yet another death at his feet in a few hours.

Everyone met at the venue in the afternoon, sitting around the table. They feasted and drank wine. Even Bjarne drank, but he still drank The normal wine. When it was time for the wedding to start. A band of great musicians played amazing music, and the food still sat at the long table. Everyone had wine cups in their hands, including King Bjarne, who began to sip on the hemlock wine that would soon be his downfall. As the wedding continued, Kaito walked down the aisle and stood at the altar in the middle, and then came to the bride, Lady Liv, who walked down to the altar in the middle.

It was time for them to say their vows.

"I, Kaito Harayuma of the kingdom Ember Fall, doth take thee, Lady Olivia, to be mine lawfully wedded wife. In the presence of our kin and under the watchful gaze of the heavens, I pledge unto thee my love, my strength, and my unwavering devotion. I shall stand by thy side in times of triumph and in times of tribulation. I vow to cherish and honor thee, to protect and support thee, and to hold thee in mine heart till the end of days." Kaito exclaimed excitedly.

"I, Lady Olivia Princess of Eldandoor, doth take thee, Kaito Harayuma. wife. In the presence of to be mine lawfully wedded husband. In the sight of our loved ones and the grace of the Almighty, I give unto thee my hand and my heart. I promise to stand with thee through joy and sorrow, to share in our triumphs, and face our challenges as one. I pledge to respect and adore thee, to comfort and encourage thee, and to hold thee in mine heart till the stars cease to shine."

Kaito and Lady Liv then exchanged their rings. Kaito's ring for Lady Liv had the sigil of his kingdom on it.

"This ring once belonged to my father; he was a great and noble man, and I want you to take this ring as a token of my love for you." Kaito exclaimed.

But right as he went to put the ring on her finger, King Bjarne grabbed a knife from the table and slid his chair back.

"It is time I cut the babe from your whore stomach Lady Olivia" he lunged forwards towards Lady Liv, but Kaito blocked the knife with his hand before he could hit her. The knife sliced deep into Kaito's hand.

"What the hell, why can't I move!" Shouted Bjarne as he struggled on the ground.

"That your grace is the doing of Hemlock poisoning, just the perfect amount of hemlock in your wine, and you are paralyzed from the legs down." Now, I want you to watch as I marry my new queen and you suffer through it. I'm sure the pain within is terrible. The crushing sensation on your legs must hurt." Kaito said, sliding the finger into Lady Liv's hand.

"This ring belonged to my mother years ago. It has been passed down from generation to generation. And it is now time you take it as a token of my unwavering love for you." Lady Liv exclaimed as she put the ring on Kaito's bloody hand.

"You may now kiss the bride." Cassius said right before Kaito and Lady Liv began to kiss.

"You two are evil, truly evil people!" Bjarne exclaimed, shouting at Kaito and Liv.

Lady Liv grabbed a dagger and opened Bjarne's mouth.

"Stick out your tongue." Liv shouted in the face of Bjarne.

Cassius was so angered he dug his nails into his hand, once again leaving blood to run from his hand. After some struggle, he finally accepted his fate. His tongue was cut from his mouth and then shoved back down his throat. Leaving Bjarne to choke on his tongue.

"Now it is time for my gift to you, your grace." Cassius said, sticking his hand out for Kaito to shake.
Kaito put his hand in, with blood still running down it. And Cassius had blood running down his as well.

"With this handshake. I grant you and your bloodline immortality. May you use this power wisely, or else bad things will-" Cassius started, but he began to feel something tearing at his stomach. A large lump began to grow out of his stomach, growing larger and larger. And then it got to his mouth. A long black arm stuck out of his mouth, grabbed his lower jaw, and snapped it forward. Another arm appeared. And then a leg shoved through his stomach. And yet another leg. And with one vicious movement Cassius's body was ripped limb from limb as a twelve-foot tall, long, matte black figure with purple eyes came out of him.

"Your world will fall, fall at the feet of your people. All because you all want power and fame. There will never be such a thing of peace after this. Nor will there be war because Desolation is among men. You will all die pitiful deaths; you will know when the time is nigh, the night will be long and cold. "YOU ARE THE KING OF DESOLATION."

The figure, who is thought to be Thornos, disappeared into a large collum of smoke into the sky. Disappearing, leaving Bjarne's body and Cassius's bodies both bleeding and lying at the feet of the true king and Queen.

Kaito looked over his loyal servants. And walked through the large puddle of blood to kiss his bride once more. After kissing his bride, he grabbed her hand and said.

"This was a great marriage between two great families… now that this is out of the way, it seems we have a greater problem on our hands." Kaito chuckled to himself. "I do not mean the desolation, no. I am talking about the birth of my child." Kaito put his hands over Liv's belly. "In this stomach lies the true heir to the realm of Nastomar. We must protect this babe at whatever cost. He is your prince, even if he has not been born yet. Do you understand me?" Kaito looked at the crowd of people surrounding him and chuckled. "Now, get these two disgusting bodies away from me. The dragon needs her part of the feast after all."

Liv chuckled and grabbed onto Kaito's arm as Oswald dragged Bjarne's body away, and Algar drug Cassius's body.

Inessa, the dragon, shocked her prey until it was cooked through and through. It was almost burnt. Kaito and now Queen Olivia stared at the sight of a young dragon devouring their enemies.